DEV FOREST

A CUSP Files Novella

ANTHONY M.STRONG

WEST
STREET

ALSO BY ANTHONY STRONG

THE JOHN DECKER SUPERNATURAL THRILLER SERIES

Soul Catcher (prequel) • What Vengeance Comes • Cold Sanctuary
Crimson Deep • Grendel's Labyrinth • Whitechapel Rising
Black Tide • Ghost Canyon • Cryptic Quest • Last Resort
Dark Force • A Ghost of Christmas Past • Deadly Crossing
Final Destiny • Night Wraith

THE CUSP FILES SERIES

Deadly Truth • Devil's Forest

THE REMNANTS SERIES

The Remnants of Yesterday • The Silence of Tomorrow

STANDALONE BOOKS

The Haunting of Willow House • Crow Song

AS A.M. STRONG WITH SONYA SARGENT

PATTERSON BLAKE FBI MYSTERY SERIES

Never Lie To Me • Sister Where Are You • Is She Really Gone

All The Dead Girls • Never Let Her Go • Dark Road From Sunset

DEVIL'S
FOREST

West Street Publishing

This is a work of fiction. Characters, names, places, and events are products of the author's imagination. Any similarity to events or places, or real persons, living or dead, is purely coincidental.

Cover art and interior design by Bad Dog Media, LLC.

ISBN: 978-1-942207-49-8

PROLOGUE

THE FLAMES of a recently built campfire warmed the cool fall air of a New England night. The flickering glow pushed back the shadows and sent long forks of dancing orange light through the trees and into the woods beyond the clearing.

Around the fire sat three men wearing thick shirts and jackets. They drank cans of beer and talked, the conversation becoming more raucous as the alcohol flowed more freely.

"This is the spot then, eh?" William Bartram—known as Big Willie to those few close friends that dared reference the six-foot-four, three-hundred-pound lumber mill worker in such a familial way—glanced around the clearing with a mixture of disdain and disappointment on his face. "The way you talk about it, I expected something a bit creepier."

"It's a forest clearing in back-of-beyond Maine thirty minutes before midnight. It's pitch black, and I've heard at least a dozen coyotes. There's no one else for fifty miles in any direction. How much creepier do you want it to get?" asked Barry Norwood, who was a foot shorter than his companion and half his weight. He also worked at the lumber mill, but in the office.

"And we're almost out of beer," said the third man, Jamie Dylan, tossing his empty can into the blackness beyond the fire and reaching into the red cooler at his side for a new one. "Don't forget that fact."

"See, now it just got way more scary." Willie chuckled to himself.

"All right, you guys. Enough. You're the ones that wanted to come up here. Honestly, I don't know why I let you talk me into it. I hate this place. You know that. Have done ever since I was a kid."

"Yeah, yeah. So you say." Willie shook his head. "Tell us the story. You were what, ten years old?"

"Twelve."

"You sure you're remembering it right?" Willie crumpled his can, then rooted in the cooler for a replacement. "You probably just saw a bear or something. You know there are more black bears in Maine than in any other state, right?"

"I remember it well enough. I know what I saw." Barry glared at his friend. "It wasn't a bear."

"I had a close call with a bear once," Jamie said. "Dang thing came right up into my backyard while I was grilling. Scared the bejesus out of me, and I don't mind admitting it."

"I'm surprised it had any interest," Willie said. "I've been to your cookouts. They're not so much a meal as a cremation."

"That was one time."

"One time too many," grumbled Willy. He turned his attention back to Barry. "I think it's about time you told us the story. You've been avoiding it all night."

"I've told you at least a dozen times already. You must know it by heart."

"You haven't told it to us around a campfire in the place where it happened."

"I thought we had a deal. If I came up here camping with you guys, we wouldn't keep talking about it. You know it freaks me out."

"And we won't," Willie said with a lopsided grin. "After you tell us the story. Now spill it."

Jamie nudged his friend. "You might as well get on with it. He isn't going to take no for an answer."

"I can see that." Barry sighed. "But then we talk about something else, okay?"

Willie shrugged.

"I'll take that as a yes." Barry took a deep breath and gathered his thoughts. "What I'm about to tell you happened back when I was a kid. My dad loved camping. Made me go with him anytime he could. He thought it was some kind of father-son bonding thing. I would have preferred to stay home, where it was warm and dry. I was never much for the outdoors—"

"Still aren't, judging by how long it took you to light that fire earlier," Willie quipped. "The bear could have done it quicker."

"Do you want to hear this or not?"

"You know I do."

"Then stop interrupting."

Willie remained quiet and sipped his beer.

"That's better," Barry said. "Now, where was I? . . . Oh yes. My dad. So anyway, he drags me up here unannounced on this weekend camping trip. Made me walk eight miles up the trail because he wanted to camp in his favorite spot where he and my grandpa always camped when he was a kid. It didn't matter that there were better campsites lower down. The first night wasn't so bad. I was exhausted after the walk, chopping wood for the fire, and catching fish in the brook to cook over it. Fell asleep in the tent before my head even hit the pillow . . ."

"So it's your dad we have to blame for our sore feet," Jamie said. "That walk hasn't gotten any shorter or easier in the years since."

"If anything, it's worse now," Barry replied. "I don't remember it being so overgrown when I came up here with my dad."

"We're getting off track again," Willie said. He leaned close to the fire and warmed his hands.

"Sorry. Anyway, that first night I was so tired. I fell asleep within moments of crawling into my sleeping bag. But I didn't sleep for long, because something paid a visit to our camp. I heard it moving around out near the campfire."

"What did you do?" asked Willie, loving the tale.

"Well, I woke my dad, and—"

"Hush." Jamie held up a hand.

"What are you doing?" Willie glared at him. "Why are you interrupting?"

"I heard a noise." Jamie looked around with wide eyes. He set his beer can down and stood up. "I swear, it sounded like something was moving out in the woods. Something big."

"Very funny." Willie swatted at his friend with a meaty hand. "Sit your ass back down. I want to hear the rest of the story."

"I'm not joking. I really heard something."

"Sure you did. I bet—"

A sharp crack came from the woods to their left, like someone standing on a fallen tree branch and snapping it underfoot.

All three men heard it this time.

"Told you." There was indignation in Jamie's voice, along with something else. A barely perceptible tremble. "There's something out there."

"I knew we shouldn't have come up here." Barry was on his feet now, too.

"The two of you are acting like a pair of schoolgirls." Willie didn't look phased. Instead, he gulped his beer. "We just got through saying these woods are full of bears. One of 'em probably got curious. Nothing to worry about. It won't come any closer, not with the fire."

"You really think it's a bear?" Jamie looked hopeful.

"What else would it be?" Willie scoffed. "The mythical beastie from Barry's story come to pay him a second visit?"

Before anyone could answer, another twig snapped. This time, it was closer.

Jamie took a step backward toward the campfire.

A deep, rumbling growl wafted from the darkness between the trees.

"That was no damned bear," Jamie said, backing closer still to the fire.

Willie wasn't so easily perturbed. He stood up with a weary sigh, reached toward the campfire, and plucked out a thick branch, flaming at one end. He brandished it like a torch. "For Pete's sake, I'm out here with a pair of sissies."

"What are you doing?" Barry asked.

"Getting rid of that bear." Willie took a step toward the tree line. "As I said, they don't like fire. Time to teach some respect."

"Don't go out there." Barry's eyes flew wide. "Are you insane?"

"You just wait here," he said with a slight slur of inebriation to his voice. "I'll take care of it. Then we can get back to polishing off the beer." He stepped from the clearing and was soon lost to the gloom among the trees.

Barry and Jamie exchanged a nervous glance.

For a moment all was silent, save for the rustle of undergrowth as Willie tromped around in the dark forest beyond the clearing. Once or twice, they glimpsed his makeshift flaming torch between the trees, the glow from which was already dying as the branch struggled to stay alight.

Then there was nothing.

"Where did he go?" Jamie asked, peering out into the forest.

"Beats me." Barry had no intention of going to look for him. Big Willie could take care of himself well enough, even against a five-hundred-pound bear. "But I know one thing, I sure as hell am not—"

Willie's scream cut Barry off mid-sentence.

Both men backpedaled instinctively toward the fire.

The scream faded away to be replaced by an even worse quietude. Not even the crickets were making a noise. It was like the woodland was holding its breath, waiting to see what would happen next.

Then, moving against the darkness between the trees, Barry caught sight of something that made the blood in his veins turn to ice. A hulking, powerful form that he recognized only too well. A monster that might as well have come from his fevered childhood nightmares.

Beside him, Jamie let out a gasp of disbelief. "Is that what I . . ." His voice trailed off as he watched the creature turn and move deeper into the forest without a backward glance. "Did we just see a Bigfoot?"

ONE

JOHN DECKER MOVED DOWN the dimly lit hallway with a catlike stealth, senses on high alert. It was midnight, a time when the occupants of the Wilmer Ridge Hotel should all be sleeping. And most of them were, except for Decker.

He came to the main staircase, a sweeping dark oak masterpiece of Victorian craftsmanship that all but cascaded from the second-floor landing to the wide lobby below. It was here, on her wedding night a century ago, that Kathryn Wilmot had tripped and tumbled to her death wearing the silk and lace evening gown she had changed into minutes before. The young woman had died right there at the bottom of the stairs, suffering a broken neck in front of her new husband, who was waiting to escort her into the ballroom, where a party was raging in their honor. Ever since, it was said, the hapless bride wandered the hotel's corridors and rooms, bereft and lost. And accompanying her ghost came the smell of violets, a lingering scent of the perfume she was wearing.

But the Woman in the White Dress, as she was known,

wasn't the only specter to haunt the elegant old hotel sitting in the shadow of Colorado's Rocky Mountains. There were plenty of people who checked in but never checked out. Like the unfortunate gambler caught cheating at cards in the hotel's smoking parlor a couple of years after it opened and took a bullet to the chest for his troubles. Then there was Delia Pickett, an up-and-coming young jazz pianist and singer from Los Angeles booked to play the hotel for a three-night engagement in the 1930s. Except she ended up murdered instead. Stabbed to death in room twenty-six, the very accommodation John Decker had requested when he booked his stay.

Her killer was never caught and Delia's spirit, like those of the unfortunate bride and the less than honest gambler, remained. On certain nights, so the story said, she still visited the room where she died or played the grand piano in the hotel bar, giving a performance in death that she had been denied in life.

And she had visited Decker that very night, not twenty minutes before, appearing at the end of his bed before vanishing right before his eyes. And if that wasn't enough, Delia had apparently made her way to the piano, where right now she was giving a ghostly performance.

Decker made his way down the stairs. The faint sound of piano music from the hotel bar growing louder as he descended. A tune he didn't recognize in a minor key with syncopated offbeat notes. It sounded exactly like something a jazz pianist from the 1930s would play. But when he crossed the lobby floor and stepped into the bar, the music stopped as abruptly as it had begun.

Decker came to a halt. Silence hung around him like a heavy blanket. If the ghostly jazz musician was still there, she was doing a good job of hiding. But he was sure the music had come from the piano. He weaved his way past empty tables toward the instrument which stood roped off in a corner of the room.

He ducked under the barrier, ignoring a 'do not touch' sign hanging from the red rope, and approached the piano. The fall board was up, the keys visible. He pressed on. A single sharp note rang out. The piano's 'voice' sounded just like that of the music he had heard when ascending the stairs, but then again, he was hardly an expert. And it didn't prove anyone had been playing mere moments before.

Decker moved to the side of the instrument. The top board was up and folded back to reveal the dampers, tuning pins, strings, and gold-colored cast-iron plate.

Peering down into the body of the instrument, Decker looked for anything out of place. He was no expert, but even to the untrained eye, it didn't look like a player piano. There was no obvious mechanism that would allow it to be operated without a pianist. Which left two options. Either the ghostly Delia Pickett really had been performing for him, or the piano music had come from somewhere else. But where? The piano case contained nothing untoward, at least as far as Decker could tell. He completed a circle around the instrument, looking for anything that might explain the phantom music. Then he ducked down and studied the underside of the piano. And that's when he found it.

There, pushed up into a recessed space below the piano's main body behind the keyboard were two small black speaker units connected by a thin strand of speaker wire which continued on down the piano's front leg to the floor where it disappeared under the bar's dark red carpet. The whole setup was practically invisible and would not be noticed by anyone who wasn't looking underneath the instrument.

Decker followed the slight bulge created by the wire as it ran underneath the carpet toward the bar area where it reappeared. The wire ran up the inside of the bar and across the back of a shelf before disappearing into a small hole drilled through the wall. Next to this was a door set into the back of the bar. When Decker tried the handle, he discovered it was unlocked.

Stepping inside, he found himself in a stockroom with bottles of liquor and wine on wire rack shelves. Several kegs of beer were stacked against the back wall. And there was something else, too. A desk with a laptop sitting on it. The wire ran across the floor to the desk where it connected to the laptop's headphone jack. He touched a key to wake the machine up. It didn't have a lock screen. Instead, he found a media player with a file loaded and ready to go. When he pressed play, the music started again out in the bar. But that wasn't all of it. Another wire from one of the computer's USB ports disappeared up into the ceiling. He had a hunch regarding where it went.

Stepping out of the stockroom and back into the bar, Decker approached the open double doors leading to the lobby. And there, mounted inconspicuously facing the doors, was a small motion sensor. This was why the music had stopped on his approach. The motion sensor had picked up movement and sent a signal to the laptop, cutting off the ghostly music lest anyone investigate and realize there was nothing otherworldly about it.

Decker had his answers. He started back toward the stairs, intending to return to his room, but at that moment, a voice boomed out.

TWO

HALF A CONTINENT AWAY, Cameron Burke—Cam to his friends—parked next to the building that housed the College of Arts and Humanities on the Central Maine University campus. He took a deep breath and gathered his nerve.

In the passenger seat, Addie Wells peered through the windshield at the dark and empty campus with a frown on her face. "Are you sure we should be doing this?"

"We don't have any choice. Professor Calloway keeps everything locked in his office desk. I can hardly just walk in there during the day."

"I don't get it. You're on his research team. He must have shared the materials with you. Why do we even need to break in?"

"We've been through this already. He doesn't let us make copies or take anything out of the lecture hall. We're not even allowed to take our phones out while we're working. Besides, I haven't seen it all. Trust me, this is the only way."

"I still don't see why we have to do it right now."

"Because I'm not the only one who's figured out the location. Marcus knows, too, but hasn't said anything yet. I'm sure of it. I don't want him to get there first." Cam glanced at his watch. It was two in the morning, and they were the only vehicle in the parking lot, which meant they would be conspicuous if one of the campus security guards in their fake police cars came cruising by. Cam unbuckled his seatbelt and pushed open the driver's door. "I'm going inside. You can stay here if you want."

"Are you crazy? I'm not sitting out here on my own."

"Fine. Then come with me. But hurry up." Cam closed his door softly and glanced around to make sure they were still alone. Then he started across the parking lot toward the building at a fast pace and walked up to the main doors, removing a key card from his pocket. As a graduate student researcher, Cam had twenty-four-hour access to most of the buildings on campus. In truth, pretty much everyone at the college had round-the-clock access.

Addie hurried behind, running to catch up. "Wait. What if Professor Calloway notices someone was poking around his office after hours? All he'd have to do is check the entry logs to know it was you."

"Don't worry. He won't know we were in his office. I'm not stealing anything. I'll copy what I need. And even if he found out, he won't trace it back to us." Cam swiped the key card and waited for the door to unlock with a soft buzz. He pushed it open and stepped inside, then turned to Addie, holding the key card up. "This isn't mine. I was in Caleb's dorm room earlier and his card was on the desk."

"You took it?"

"Borrowed it." Cam turned and walked through the lobby toward a set of stairs leading to the second floor where the faculty offices were located and started up. "I'll put it back where I found it. If he notices it missing before that, he'll just think it's lost."

"This is getting out of hand." Addie glanced around nervously. Because it was after midnight, the building was illuminated by dim auxiliary lighting that cast long shadows down the stairwell. She shuddered and picked up the pace, almost bumping into Cam at the top in her eagerness to get off the stairs. "How are you going to get into Calloway's office? I'm sure he keeps it locked after hours."

"No problem." Cam grinned. "This is one of the oldest buildings on campus. They never bothered putting key cards on the office doors."

"Please tell me you didn't steal the professor's keys."

"I'm not stupid." Cam reached into his pocket and removed a couple of paperclips. "I watched a video on lock picking. Shouldn't be all that hard."

Addie rolled her eyes. "You can't be serious. This is a waste of time. We should go back to the car."

"Hey. I can do this. I practiced on my dorm room door earlier."

"Is that why you were late picking me up for dinner?"

"No." Cam shook his head. "I was having a few beers with the guys after class. That's why I was in Caleb's room."

"There's no way you're going to pick that lock, internet video or otherwise. You're a history student, not a burglar."

"Watch me." Cam approached the door to the professor's office. He bent low and studied the lock for a moment before straightening one end of each paperclip. He inserted one into the bottom of the lock and pulled it down to apply tension. "They call this a torque wrench in the video."

"It's a paperclip . . . And you're a dork." Addie glanced down the corridor, half expecting to see a campus security guard approaching them. "This is ridiculous."

"You won't be saying that when we get what we came for."

"Just hurry. The quicker you realize a couple of old paperclips won't open that door, the sooner we can get out of here."

"Oh, yea of little faith." Cam grinned. He pushed the other paperclip into the top of the lock and jiggled it around. "This acts as the pick."

Addie shook her head and watched her boyfriend poke and prod the paperclip in the door lock. After about a minute, he let out a muttered curse. She grinned. "Not as easy as you thought, huh?"

"Give me another moment. I've almost got it." Cam pushed the paperclip deep into the top of the lock one more time. Then there was an audible click. He twisted the door handle and pushed the door open with a flourish. "Voilà."

"Alright, I take it back. You're the Houdini of CMU."

"Houdini was an escape artist."

"He still picked locks," Addie said, following Cam into the office and closing the door again. "Stop splitting hairs. What are we looking for, anyway?"

"A bundle of papers."

"Great. That won't take long." Addie looked around in dismay. The room was lined with shelves stacked high with old books, paperwork, and file folders, some of which looked like they hadn't been moved in a decade. "This guy has more old papers than the national archives."

"He's a history professor. What do you expect?" Cam went to the desk and sat behind it, then pulled open a drawer. "Help me look. He keeps the papers in a big manila envelope."

"Still no help." Addie searched the shelves to her right while Cam continued rifling through the desk.

A couple of minutes later, while she was leafing through a stack of exam papers, Cam let out a triumphant exclamation. "Found it."

"Thank heavens for that." Addie turned toward the desk. "Can we get out of here now?"

"Sure. Just as soon as I copy these." Cam spread the papers over the desk, then pulled his phone out. He snapped several pictures, photographing each document, then put his phone away, bundled the papers together again, before slipping them back into the drawer where he had found them. "Okay. Done."

"Great." Addie moved toward the door. She reached for the handle, was about to turn it, then pulled her hand away in surprise. From the other side of the door came the distinct sound of heavy footsteps echoing down the corridor.

THREE

"HEY, what the hell do you think you're doing?"

Decker turned to see a thin, balding man with spectacles crossing the lobby. It was the hotel manager. Why he was around at such an ungodly hour was anyone's guess, except maybe because he had a hand in the evening's paranormal activities.

"I was just admiring your little ghost set up," Decker said. "You've got quite the theatrical performance going on here."

"You have no right to be snooping around here," the manager replied, clearly trying to sound authoritative but failing. "Going into areas that are off-limits to our guests. I could have you thrown out of the hotel."

"But you won't." Decker kept moving toward the stairs and started up, aware that the manager was scurrying along behind. "Because it will bring too much attention to your dubious marketing efforts. I bet you would get a lot less people in this place if they knew it isn't really haunted."

"Now, listen here. Guest experiences are subjective. We don't specifically state that the hotel is haunted."

Decker was at the top of the stairs now. He turned to face the manager. "You literally claim your hotel is haunted on the front page of your website. You have flyers in the local tourist information office saying the same thing. Besides, you were more than happy to book me into the Delia Pickett room when I made my reservation, knowing full well that I have an interest in such phenomena."

"That's because you told me you were a producer for The Unexplained Channel, considering us for an episode of Extreme Ghost Haunts. You weren't supposed to go sniffing around, debunking the legends about this place. Are you even with The Unexplained Channel?"

"Why don't you call them in the morning and ask?" Decker made his way down the corridor to his room and let himself in. "In the meantime, I'm going back to bed, and hopefully Delia Pickett's ghost won't make another appearance. If she does, I'm unplugging the projector."

"I don't know what you're talking about." The hotel manager stood in the doorway with his arms folded.

Decker turned to him and pointed to a mirror hanging on the wall opposite the bed and secured by screws. "Really? I bet if I took that mirror down, I'd find a projector behind it." He motioned toward the bed. A four-poster with white decorative netting hanging from the top bar down beyond the footboard. "The glass acts as a rear projection screen. In a dark room it gives the illusion of a ghostly entity hovering at the end of the bed. Victorian theaters used a similar trick to create ghosts by projecting an image onto a sheet of glass between the audience and the actors. Gave me quite a start until I realized it was nothing more than a cheap parlor trick."

"You touch that mirror and I'll bill you for the damage." The hotel manager did not look impressed. "Thank goodness you didn't wake any of the other guests."

"I'm sure they are all safely tucked up, enjoying whatever ghostly shenanigans you've cooked up for them." Decker yawned. "Now if you don't mind . . ."

The manager eyed Decker warily. "If one word of this affair ends up on your TV channel, I'll sue you and your employer for defamation. You mark my words."

"And you would lose," Decker said, taking the door and closing it on the blustering hotel manager, causing him to step back quickly. Then he turned back to the bed and undressed for the second time that night. Fifteen minutes later, he was sound asleep.

FOUR

"THERE'S someone out in the corridor." Addie turned to Cam and spoke in a low tone. "We're going to get caught."

Cam approached the door and listened. "It's fine. Probably just another student looking for somewhere to do some late-night studying. Keep quiet and we'll be fine."

"Or it could be campus security." Addie cursed her own stupidity. She should never have let Cam talk her into this. It was a bad idea, and she knew it. Even if it was just a professor's office, it was still breaking and entering. They could get kicked out of school. Cam could lose his graduate assistant job.

"Only one way to find out." Cam gripped the door handle and turned it, opening the door a crack.

"What are you doing?"

"Hush." Cam peered through the gap, then he closed the door quickly and backed away from the door. "We have to find a place to hide. Right now."

"What? Why?" Addie looked around, frantic. There was

nowhere in the small office to conceal themselves except behind the desk, and that was hardly a good hiding place.

"We must have tripped an alarm when we broke in here. There's an entire SWAT team outside. They're going to kick the door in at any moment."

Addie took a quick step further into the office, then she realized Cam was bent over laughing. Her cheeks flushed hot. She swiped him. "You're an ass."

"I'm sorry," Cam sputtered, straightening up. "You're so nervous. It was too good an opportunity to pass up."

Addie glared at him.

Cam had recovered his composure now. "We're safe. It was just a couple of students heading down from the third floor. They probably snuck up onto the roof to make out or something."

"Can we go now?"

"Sure." Cam cracked the door open again and peered out into the corridor. "Coast is clear."

"Great." Addie pushed the door wider and stepped out of the office, then started down the corridor toward the stairs. "You coming?"

"Hang on. I have to lock the door again." Cam turned the knob on the inside of the door to set the lock and pulled it closed. Then he ran to catch up. "You're staying over tonight, right?" He asked hopefully as he drew level with her.

"I was going to. Now I'm not so sure."

"Come on. It was just a joke." Cam nudged Addie playfully.

"To you, maybe. I'm not even sure I want to go on your weekend trip anymore."

"Don't say that. I need your help. Besides, you'll enjoy it. A couple of nights together in a tent with no one around."

"In the middle of the Maine wilderness during winter. It's

going to be freezing up there." Addie started down the stairs toward the lobby.

"I'll keep you warm." Cam's eyes sparkled with anticipation. "We can share a sleeping bag."

"We'll see." Addie was at the bottom of the stairs now. She walked across the lobby and pulled the main doors open. A chill wind whipped through the opening, making her shudder. Cam's Volkswagen looked like an island of warmth sitting alone in the dark and empty parking lot. She stepped outside, waited for Cam, then let the doors close behind them.

He put an arm around her. "I really am sorry. No more pranks."

"Good." Addie returned the hug and gave him a quick kiss. Then she broke away and headed toward the car at a fast pace.

Cam lingered a moment, looking around, then descended the steps and followed. "Does this mean you'll come back to my place tonight?"

Addie glanced back over her shoulder with a grin, and for the second time in as many minutes, she said, "We'll see!"

FIVE

DECKER'S PHONE rang at six in the morning. And not his personal phone, but the secure handset given to him by his employer, Classified Universal Special Projects, or CUSP as they were more often referred to, at least to those who knew of their existence. He reached out, groggy, and answered it with a gruff, "Yes?"

"It's me," came the terse reply.

"Adam." Decker pushed himself up at the sound of his superior's voice. "Do you have any idea what time it is?"

"Obviously."

"Then why are you calling at such an ungodly hour?"

"It's eight A.M. here on the East Coast."

"Right. But it's only six here, and I was up half the night chasing ghosts." Decker considered telling Hunt to call back in a couple of hours, hang up, and go back to sleep, but thought better of it. Yet even for his boss, a man not known for his thoughtfulness and empathy, this was a bit much. "What is it you want?"

"Well, for a start, how about you fill me in on your little

ghost hunting adventure. Is the Wilmer Ridge Hotel the real deal?"

"Not even close," Decker said, swinging his legs off the bed and slipping from under the covers. He wasn't going to get any more sleep. That much was obvious. "The place is nothing but a tourist trap with some cleverly concocted although dubiously moral special effects meant to mislead guests into believing they're really staying in a haunted hotel. Hidden projectors. Cleverly concealed speakers. Lights rigged to flicker. Artificial cold spots. It's all designed to play on the fame of the much more well-known haunted hotel not far from here. I can't say one way or the other if there are any genuine ghosts wandering around Wilmer Ridge, but if so, those entities are being overshadowed by the rather blatant fakery."

"Shame. After all the press that hotel has gotten, I thought we might be dealing with real paranormal events."

"Sorry to disappoint you." Decker went to the window, opened the curtains, and looked out toward the Rocky Mountains beyond the resort grounds. Soon the sun would set the horizon ablaze as it rose above the peaks to start a new day, but right now, the landscape was still wrapped in darkness. He had to admit, the out-of-the-way hotel provided a suitably creepy atmosphere, even if the reality was disappointing. "Short of providing inspiration for any horror writers who happen to wander through, there's not much here."

"At least we did our due diligence." If Hunt was disappointed, it didn't show in his voice. "And it's fortuitous that you've wrapped up your investigation because I need you elsewhere. Something's come up."

"I still have another night booked here, but I can check out early. Probably for the best." Decker wasn't sure he would still have a room, anyway, given the hotel manager's animosity toward him. "Want to fill me in?"

"I've sent the relevant details to your email, but I can give you the short version." Hunt cleared his throat. "A group of campers out in the Maine wilderness claim to have encountered a Sasquatch."

"Bigfoot?" Decker closed the curtains and turned away from the window. "Hasn't CUSP investigated those before and come up empty?"

"We have. That doesn't mean the creature is any less real. We just haven't gotten lucky and found one . . . yet."

"And you think this is our opportunity?"

"Maybe. I would usually dismiss the claims of a bunch of guys who went up into the woods and got drunk around a campfire, but in this case, there's physical evidence . . . of sorts."

"Proof of a Bigfoot? This should be good."

"I wouldn't go as far as calling it proof. But something happened up in those woods. The campers were attacked by what they claim to be Bigfoot. One of the three was injured. Those injuries are consistent with an animal attack. Something large and powerful."

"Probably a bear," Decker said. "I wouldn't be surprised if the misidentification of bears could explain at least some Bigfoot sightings."

"I agree. But in this case, I'm not so sure. The man who was attacked pulled out several of the creature's hairs during the struggle. He was still gripping them when he went to the hospital. We obtained those hairs and ran DNA analysis."

"And?"

"They came back inconclusive. There was no match with any known primate in our databases. Even the more *unusual* ones like those we keep in the Zoo. Now, that still doesn't prove we're dealing with a Sasquatch, but it does discount the bear theory."

"Unless the sample was contaminated." Despite everything Decker had seen, he still liked to play devil's advocate once in a while. During his days as a cop, he'd learned not to jump to conclusions based on assumptions. Still, Hunt was right. It was unusual. Especially since the samples didn't match anything in the sprawling containment facility known as the Zoo that was hidden underneath CUSP's headquarters. A facility that housed many of the more dangerous creatures the organization had dealt with.

"The sample wasn't contaminated."

"Okay. I'll take your word for that." Decker was already pulling his travel bag out of the hotel room's small closet. "I assume you have a flight booked for me?"

"I do. You're booked on a ten-thirty morning flight out of Denver to Boston. From there, you'll pick up a rental car and head north to Bangor. It's a four-hour drive. Another operative named Theo Levesque is already waiting at a local motel along with all the gear you'll need. I sent you the address. I've also assigned you a Ghost Team escort for security. Philip Strand. He's a good man. Any trouble, and he's got your back."

"Glad to hear it," Decker said. "What happens after that?"

"You'll stay overnight and rendezvous the next morning with Barry Norwood, one of the three campers who got attacked. Norwood will lead you to their campsite. You'll be driving through Portland, so feel free to stop by your house and pick up fresh clothes and anything else you'll need for a trek into the woods. But make it quick."

"No worries." Decker and Nancy had moved to Portland, Maine, a few months before to be close to CUSP's headquarters on a remote island off the coast. He had been looking forward to going home and spending a few days with Nancy. Now it would have to wait. "I'll check in with you when I get to Boston."

"I'll be waiting." Hunt hesitated a moment. "And John, good job disproving that haunted hotel. One less thing for us to deal with."

"All in a day's work," Decker said, before saying goodbye and hanging up. Then he packed his belongings, checked out of the hotel, and was on the road heading for Denver an hour later.

SIX

THE FLIGHT from Denver to Boston took off sixty minutes late. Decker settled into his seat and waited until they were airborne, then took out his laptop and read over the information Adam Hunt had sent him via email. The report elaborated on the information Hunt had already provided when he called earlier in the day.

The man he was traveling to meet, Barry Norwood, along with two friends, were camping in the wilderness when they were attacked by what he claimed was a large and aggressive hominid. One of the three, a big man in his own right, had engaged the creature in the woods near their camp, suffering two broken ribs, a dislocated shoulder, and a fractured skull in the process. After that, the creature prowled around for over an hour, hassling the terrified campers at intervals until it eventually lost interest and disappeared back into the forest. At that point, Norwood and his friend carried their injured colleague out on a jury-rigged stretcher constructed from tree limbs and a piece of canvas cut from one of their tents. Then they hiked back down the trail, carrying the wounded man between them. A journey that had taken them almost an entire day.

Decker looked up from the laptop as a pair of flight attendants came down the aisle pushing a refreshment cart. When they drew close, he closed the laptop and accepted a can of soda. He poured the drink into a plastic tumbler filled with ice and drank it slowly, then glanced at his watch. Three more hours of flight time. He briefly considered reading over the assignment details again but decided against it. There was nothing more he could glean from the briefly worded email.

After returning the laptop to his carry-on bag stowed under his seat, Decker settled back and closed his eyes. He'd barely gotten four hours of sleep the night before thanks to Adam Hunt's early morning call, and he wanted to be refreshed for the drive north to Bangor later that day. Soon, he fell into a fitful sleep despite the turbulence that rocked the cabin as they flew over the mountains, and the plaintive wail of an unhappy toddler seated several rows back.

The plane landed three hours later. While they were waiting to disembark, he called Adam Hunt and checked in, then grabbed his carry-on bag, waited for the throng of passengers ahead of him to clear the aisle, and made his way to the car-rental desk where he picked up a rugged Jeep Wrangler. He didn't stop by the luggage carousel because there was nothing to collect. Decker preferred to travel light, especially when he was on shorter domestic assignments.

When Decker left the airport, he immediately hit rush hour traffic. The thirty-minute drive out of the city took almost three times as long. By the time he reached Portland and parked up outside the house he and Nancy had purchased a few months before, his nerves were frazzled, and he was ready for a break. He was also hoping to see Nancy, but her car was gone. She was probably out shopping or looking for a location in which to house the bakery and coffee shop she had been planning ever since they moved north. He almost sent her a text but changed his mind. He didn't have the time. Instead, he grabbed his bag from the back seat of the Jeep and let himself into the house. Going upstairs to the bedroom, he ditched his old clothes, throwing them in the laundry basket, and packed new ones. Going downstairs, he went to the den and a concealed wall safe behind the desk. Inside was his Glock pistol, which he put into the bag along with a box of ammo. Then he returned to the Jeep, deposited the bag on the back seat, climbed in, and drove north toward Bangor.

SEVEN

IT WAS eleven P.M. by the time Decker arrived at the hotel in Bangor. The men he was there to meet, Theo Levesque and Philip Strand, had already checked in hours before. After picking up his room key from reception and dropping his bag off, Decker went to Levesque's room and introduced himself.

Theo Levesque was a wiry French-Canadian. A zoologist recruited to CUSP the previous year, although Decker had never worked with him. This wasn't surprising. Classified Universal Special Projects had operatives around the globe, and Decker, still fairly new to the organization, had come into contact with only a handful of them.

"You're late," the zoologist said irritably in a thick Québec accent when Decker knocked on his hotel room door. "I was expecting you hours ago."

"Flight got delayed and there was traffic in Boston," Decker said, doing his best not to sound annoyed even though he found the zoologist's brusque attitude unwarranted. He took a calming breath. "I'm here now. That's all that matters."

"You'd better come in," Levesque said, stepping away from the door to allow Decker into the hotel room. "I trust Adam Hunt filled you in on why we're here."

"He did." Decker stepped into the room and stood with his arms folded. "Group of campers claim they encountered a Bigfoot."

Levesque snorted. "There's no such thing as Bigfoot."

Decker was taken momentarily aback. "I'm surprised you can say that with such authority, considering who we both work for."

"I've been on three expeditions searching for the creature, and never found a scrap of evidence that it exists. As far as I'm concerned, Bigfoot is a myth. A fairytale. Its people with overactive imaginations misidentifying other critters, or just plain seeing things in the darkness that aren't there, then getting themselves all in a tizzy."

"What about the hair sample recovered from the victim?" Decker asked.

"Doesn't prove a thing. Came back inconclusive. No match. That isn't the same thing as proving the existence of a giant hominid."

"Doesn't disprove it, either." Decker was already regretting the decision to let Levesque know he had arrived instead of waiting until morning to meet up with the rest of the team. He crossed to a table near the window and sat down, weary. "Trust me, I've seen things I would never have believed during my time as a cop in New York, but my skepticism didn't make them any less real."

Levesque took the other chair. "No offense, Mr. Decker, but unlike you, I'm a scientist. A zoologist, to be exact. The real kind that doesn't think cryptids are hiding behind every tree and rock. I deal with hard facts and proof. And for the record, I've seen my fair share of strange things, too. Sort of goes with the job. If we go up there tomorrow and come face-to-face with a Sasquatch, then I will be a believer. Until that time, I shall reserve judgment and err on the side of caution."

"Speaking of which, what time are we supposed to meet Barry Norwood, the witness?"

"Nine in the morning. Once he gets here, we'll head straight out. I trust that is agreeable to you?" Decker nodded. "According to the file Adam Hunt sent me, it's a fair trek up to the campsite."

Now it was Levesque's turn to nod. "We'll drive another three hours north toward the Canadian border and then it's a long slog on foot from there. Maybe two hours more through thick forestland that rises in elevation. The going might get tough in places. I hope you brought hiking boots and a good mountain jacket."

"I've got everything I need back in my hotel room," Decker replied. "Don't you worry about that."

"Pleased to hear it." Levesque stood up and brushed the crease from his shirt. "And now, I think it's time we got some sleep. We have an early start in the morning and our Ghost Team escort is most insistent that we leave on time."

"Philip Strand," Decker said, standing and making his way to the door. "He's a good man. I've worked with him a few times. He is a stickler for punctuality, though."

"It would seem so." Levesque didn't sound pleased. "I must confess, I would have preferred a later start, but when the Ghost Team is involved, assignments invariably end up feeling more like military operations."

Decker smirked despite himself. The same thought had crossed his own mind more than once when dealing with the Ghost Team. Thankfully, many of his assignments did not warrant such an involvement. He opened the door and stepped out. "I'll see you bright and early. Sleep tight."

"You, too," Levesque replied.

Decker turned and walked back to his room as Levesque's door clicked shut behind him. When he got inside, he took out his personal cell phone and called Nancy. They ended up talking well into the early hours.

EIGHT

WHEN DECKER EXITED his room at eight-forty-five the next morning, Theo Levesque and Philip Strand were already waiting in the parking lot. A third man was standing there with them. He was tall and broad shouldered with thinning sandy brown hair. Decker assumed this must be Barry Norwood.

He soon received confirmation when Strand introduced everyone before nodding toward a pancake restaurant sitting on an out-parcel across the parking lot near the road. "We have a long and grueling day ahead of us. We should put some fuel in our bodies before we get underway."

"Suits me," Decker said. He was starving. He followed the Ghost Team operative across the parking lot and into the restaurant, where the four of them settled into a booth near the back, as far away from the other customers as possible.

After studying the menu for a few moments, Strand laid it on the table. "I would suggest you all load up on carbs for energy. Try the multigrain French toast, or the pancakes. But don't overeat. We'll be topping up as we go to keep our energy levels where they should be."

"I'm really not that hungry," Levesque said. "Not much of a breakfast person."

"Eat something anyway." Strand glared at the zoologist across the table. "You'll regret it later if you don't."

"But—"

"It isn't a request."

Levesque opened his mouth to reply, then thought better of it. When the server returned, he ordered a stack of pancakes then sat and stared out the window with his arms folded tight across his chest.

Strand waited for the server to depart then leaned forward and fixed the rest of the group with a serious stare. He spoke in a quiet yet authoritative voice. "I want to make sure everyone understands the rules regarding our little jaunt. It's my job to keep everyone safe. When we get out there, I'm in charge. We don't know what we're going to encounter, and I intend to bring you all back alive and preferably unharmed. If I tell you to do something, you do it without question. Are we clear on that?"

"Sure." Levesque shrugged. "But I think you're being a wee bit overdramatic. It's Maine. People go hiking out in the woods all the time. It's kind of why people come here. I can't imagine anything much is going to happen except for a bug bite or two and some blisters on our feet."

"I hope you're right, but we should exercise caution, none-the-less." Strand's gaze drifted toward Norwood. "Don't forget, something put this man's friend in the hospital."

"Granted." Levesque unrolled his silverware from a white paper napkin. "And it's probably long gone by now."

"We shall see." Strand smiled slightly and glanced around.

The restaurant was getting busier by the minute. Several groups had entered, including a trio of men wearing plaid shirts and fishing vests who settled on a nearby table.

"We should keep the conversation to a minimum until we get out of here," Decker said, reading Strand's mind. "At least regarding the subject at hand."

"A wise precaution." Strand tipped his head toward Decker in acknowledgment, then he looked down at his coffee cup. "And in the meantime, if anyone happens to see our server, please flag them down. I could use a refill."

NINE

THEY DROVE north for three hours. Decker sat in the front passenger seat of Strand's Range Rover, which reminded him of the modified vehicle Colum O'Shea had driven in Ireland. There was even the mandatory hidden compartment in the trunk full of weapons that Decker hoped would not be necessary.

They left their cars parked at the hotel in Bangor, where they still had reservations for the next four nights, which Hunt deemed long enough to take care of whatever trouble they might encounter in the wilds of Maine. Not that they would be utilizing their rooms any time soon. Going back and forth was too long a drive, so they were going to pitch tents at the campsite instead. Something Hunt had forgotten to mention during his brief call at the hotel back in Colorado.

The mood in the car was tense. Norwood jiggled one leg nervously, the tick getting worse the closer they got to their destination. He stared out the window and didn't seem inclined to discuss the terrifying experience out in the woods that had brought them together. Decker decided not to push him, opting instead to let him work through his anxiety before pressing him on the matter.

Eventually, under a gray and threatening sky, they reached their destination. The small city of Caribou near the Canadian border. Strand went straight to the downtown area, found a convenience store, and pulled up out front.

"Welcome to the northernmost city in the country, boys," he said, opening his door and climbing from the vehicle. He waited for the others to join him. "We have a long hike ahead of us. Use the bathroom, grab a sandwich for the trail and any other snacks you want, and be back at the car in ten."

Decker rubbed his hands. "It's cold here."

"Forty degrees right now." Strand glanced toward the ashen sky. "Enjoy it. Temperature's going to plummet overnight. Thirty degrees if we're lucky. Might even get a sprinkling of snow."

"Wonderful." Levesque shook his head and made for the convenience store. "Maybe they have a couple extra sweaters in here, too."

"I've camped in worse." Norwood followed behind. "This ain't so bad."

"Says you." Levesque held the door open for the others to enter. "Quick tip. Next time, try to have your Bigfoot encounter in the summer."

———

Ten minutes later, right on time, they were back at the car. Strand drove a few miles out of town to a wilderness trail leading deep into the forest and parked at the trailhead in a small gravel lot. He wasted no time in distributing camping gear to each of them to carry up to the campsite. Tents. Sleeping bags. Provisions. All neatly packed in four heavy backpacks. Decker transferred his clothes and other meagre possessions from the bag he had brought with him to the one assigned to him by Strand, and then they set off for the spot where Norwood had encountered what he claimed was a Bigfoot.

At first the going was easy, but the further away from the trailhead they got, the harder the terrain became. They walked single file, with Strand taking the lead. He walked with his heavy pack on his back and a rifle slung over one shoulder. Even if they didn't run into a Bigfoot, there were other dangerous animals up here. Like black bears, bobcats, coyotes, lynx, and wolves. Norwood went second, his gaze shifting from one side of the trail to the other, as if he expected one of those beasts to lunge from the undergrowth at any moment. Or perhaps he thought a more elusive creature lurked nearby. Levesque, following third, carried a backpack over one shoulder and a sleek air rifle over the other. Inside his backpack were several tranquilizer darts, stored in a small thermal pouch chilled by dry ice. Decker bringing up the rear, kept his gaze on all of them and hoped that they wouldn't need either rifle.

"You realize it's going to be next to impossible to prove that a Bigfoot is on the lose out here," Levesque said eventually, returning to a topic that seemed to be a favorite of his. "Even if there were such a thing, the creatures are supposed to be elusive and solitary. After hundreds of years of sightings, not to mention a wealth of Native American folklore regarding Sasquatch and other apelike creatures, no one has ever captured one, found a dead body, or even found bones."

"I never said this job was easy." Decker stepped over the remains of a spindly tree that had fallen across the trail, probably during a recent downpour when the ground became sodden.

"If you ask me, it was a bear, plain and simple," Levesque said, mirroring Decker's earlier sentiment to Adam Hunt. He brushed an insect away from his face with a scowl.

"It wasn't a bear." Norwood was listening to their conversation. Now he stopped on the trail and turned to face them. "I'm a seasoned outdoorsman. I know the difference between a bear and a Bigfoot. Besides, it's not the first time I've seen one."

"All I'm saying is that—"

Norwood cut Levesque off with a shake of his head. "Don't patronize me. You people are supposed to be taking this seriously. That's what your organization promised when they approached me. I already went through enough with the police, my coworkers, and even members of my family laughing at me, telling me I don't know what I saw with my own eyes. If you're not here to help, I'm going back."

"We are taking you seriously." Decker stepped between the two men. "I can assure you of that." He turned his attention to Levesque. "Whatever attacked these men, it wasn't a bear. You read the briefing, just like me."

"And nowhere in that document did it confirm that we're dealing with a Bigfoot."

"But it did confirm that something unknown to science is up here. We have the DNA test to prove it." Decker leaned close to Levesque. "And you should be excited to discover something new. Bigfoot or otherwise."

"You're right, of course." Levesque's shoulders slumped. He looked at Norwood. "I'm sorry. I meant no offense. It is my nature to question what I can't prove and look for rational explanations. Mr. Decker has a lot of experience with the unusual and unexplained. He is, for lack of a better term, a monster hunter."

"I really hate that job title," Decker said.

"Really?" Levesque raised an eyebrow. "Because I've read some of the reports. Those that aren't super-classified. The prehistoric alligator in Florida is one of my—"

"Gentlemen." Strand was standing a few feet distant on the trail, looking uncomfortable. "Might I suggest we keep moving? We have a long way to go and still need to make camp when we arrive. We only have three hours of daylight left, and if there really is an angry Bigfoot or some other unknown creature up here, I would prefer not to be stumbling around in the forest after dark."

"You have a point," Decker said. He glanced between Levesque and Norwood. "We'll continue this conversation later when we're safe around a roaring fire."

TEN

THEY ARRIVED at the spot where Norwood claimed to have had his encounter a little after four in the afternoon, which gave them little more than an hour before the light started to wane. The campsite was nothing much to look at. Little more than an irregular shaped clearing carved out the forest with a couple of fallen logs setting the boundary and the remains of old campfires still visible in the center. The trail they had hiked in on skirted the side of the clearing and kept going higher into the wilderness.

Strand quickly made his way into the clearing and dropped his pack on the ground with obvious relief. He flexed his shoulders and turned to the rest of the group. "We have a limited amount of time to set up the tents and build a fire. I don't want to be caught in the dark. Bigfoot aside, there are other dangerous animals up here that might be attracted to our presence. Bobcats. Bears. Coyotes. The fire will keep them at a safe distance. We'll also need to find a suitable spot or two somewhere close to camp—but not too close—to do our business. We'll dig catholes unless the ground is too hard.

If that's the case, we're packing it back out in plastic bags. You have been warned."

Levesque pulled a face. "Gross. Poop pits! I hate primitive camping."

"We're not here to have fun," Strand said. "And hopefully, it will only be for a few days. You'll survive."

"I always do." Levesque dropped his bag on the ground and kneeled to unzip it. He pulled out four trail cams and laid them on the ground. "Since we're up here looking for proof of a crypto-zoological creature, I figured these would come in useful. I would have brought more, but there's only so much I can carry." He glanced toward the dense forest surrounding them. "I'd like to set these up beyond the tree line, covering the trail and any other easy access to the campsite. Hopefully, we'll catch whatever comes our way. They have superb night vision. Can pick up movement in almost total darkness."

"Just make sure you keep them pointed away from our catholes, then," Norwood said. "I'd rather not put on a show with my pants around my ankles."

"Trust me, none of us want to see that." Levesque grabbed the trail cams and stood up. He looked at Strand. "Mind if I make these a priority?"

"Go for it." Strand turned to Decker. "How are you at putting up tents?"

"I've done it once or twice."

"Good." Strand watched Levesque head off toward the forest with the trail cams cradled in his arms. "That will be our job, then."

"What about me?" Norwood asked.

"You are on campfire duty. Make a fire pit and gather enough wood to keep us going, then build a fire. Think you can handle that?"

"Give me twenty minutes and I'll have a blaze going that will keep us warm all night."

"Good man." Strand slapped Norwood on the back. He turned to Decker. "Now, how about we get those tents up and sleeping bags rolled out, so we have somewhere to sleep tonight?"

ELEVEN

IT WAS late in the evening. The sun had slipped behind the trees in a brief spectacle of fiery reds and yellows over an hour ago, and darkness encroached on all sides, pushing at the light from the campfire's leaping flames. All four men sat around the fire on collapsible camping chairs. Behind them, near the edge of the clearing, were four tents that Strand and Decker had set up while Norwood built the fire and Levesque placed the trail cams. Now, with the hard work done, Decker wanted to hear Norwood's story first-hand.

"I think it's time you tell us about the Bigfoot," Decker said, staring across the fire at Barry Norwood.

"I agree," Levesque added. "Earlier, when we were on the trail, you claimed to have seen the creature more than once."

"Unfortunately." Norwood squirmed in his seat. He looked around as if hoping someone would change the subject. When they didn't, he drew a long breath. "I was just a kid the first time I saw Bigfoot."

"Out here, in this spot?"

"Yes. Right where we're sitting." Norwood rubbed his

hands together and inched closer to the fire. "My father used to take me camping. He was into all that stuff. Fancied himself a bit of an outdoorsman and wanted to pass his legacy on to me. He dragged me up here every opportunity he could. Summer vacation. Spring break. A couple of days around Thanksgiving. Even made us camp out in the middle of winter once or twice. Only time he didn't make me go camping with him was when the snow got so deep, and the temperature dropped so low, that my mother put her foot down and said no."

"That's dedication right there." Levesque raised an eyebrow.

"Yeah. Or insanity. I couldn't have cared less about camping back then. All I wanted to do was play video games and throw a ball around with my friends, but he never gave me a choice . . ." Barry's voice trailed off. He stared into the fire.

No one spoke, perhaps sensing the tension in the air.

After a while, Barry cleared his throat and started again. "When I was twelve years old, we came up to this clearing for a weekend in October. As usual, he made me hike in with all my gear on my back, which was super heavy. Wouldn't cut me a break even though I struggled to carry it all. We made camp, got to doing the usual, none of which I particularly liked. He insisted we live off the land, so we had to catch fish from the brook half a mile to the north and chop our own firewood. The first night, as we cooked our catch over the fire, he started in as usual, telling me stories about the forest. He liked to do that. Thought it was fun to scare me. Not in a mean way or anything, mind you. I guess he figured I liked it, and I let him do it because I didn't have the heart to say how much those stories affected me. I could barely close my eyes for a week after one of his camping trips, let alone go to sleep."

"What were the stories about?" Decker asked.

"Ghosts watching us from the shadows. Werewolves prowling the woods looking for fresh victims. Escaped lunatics from the insane asylum over in Jenksville. You know, the usual campfire tales. Mostly, I knew it was hogwash. But there was this one tale he liked to tell every time we came up here. He claimed it was a true story about an encounter he had as a kid. He and my grandpa were camping in this very spot when something came out of the woods and started nosing around their tent. He said that when he looked out, there was a big hairy shape standing by the fire. Seven feet tall and stinking like a pile of rotten garbage. It looked at him and made this strange grunting sound before turning and walking off into the woods. Grandpa told him it was the Sasquatch come to steal their souls."

"Wow," Levesque said. "That story would've been enough to send me screaming all the way home. No wonder you didn't enjoy camping."

"Tell me about it," Barry said. "So, this one time when I was twelve, he started in with the stories as usual, talking in this low gravelly voice he thought made them more frightening. Hit all his favorites. The ghost of a fur trapper killed who got lost and froze to death. There were local monsters like the Shagamaw, which was supposed to be half moose and half bear, and the Agropelter, a monkey-like creature that liked to take swipes at passing lumberjacks. Myths perpetuated by loggers in the nineteenth century. Then he got around to the Sasquatch. By the time he finished, I was a nervous wreck. Kept looking out into the woods expecting to see something staring back at me. Then it was time for bed."

"That's when you had your first encounter?" Decker asked.

"Not the first night, although something did happen. I woke up a little before dawn because I heard a noise outside the tent. Like an animal moving around. It freaked me out, so I woke my dad up. He stuck his head out of the tent to look, then he told me to stay quiet. That the Bigfoot was out there. I almost puked. I was so terrified. After a while, my dad laughed and said it wasn't the Bigfoot. He was joking. It was just a big fat raccoon sniffing around the fire pit. But the damage had been done. All I could think about the next day was that hairy creature stomping around outside the tent. By the time we went to bed the next night, I convinced myself that it hadn't been a raccoon and that my dad just said that to make me feel better."

"What a nice guy," said Strand, with a shake of his head. "Traumatizing a kid like that."

"He meant nothing by it. It was just his way."

"What happened the second night?" Decker asked.

"The second night. That was worse. Much worse." Barry closed his eyes for a moment as if he were remembering something dreadful, then he continued. "It was the middle of the night. Maybe two or three in the morning. I needed to pee so bad. I didn't want to go outside alone, but I didn't want to wake my dad two nights in a row. Heaven knows, he would have told me more horror stories. So I unzipped the flap and crawled out on my own. That's when I saw it standing by the dying embers of the campfire. A beast just like the one in my father's story. It was covered in thick black hair and standing on two legs. It reeked like you can't imagine. The smell made me gag. It looked at me with glowing yellow eyes and bared its teeth."

"What did you do?" asked Levesque, enraptured despite his disbelief in such things.

"What do you think I did? I screamed and scrambled back inside the tent. That woke my father, obviously. He jumped up and ran outside, almost collapsing the tent around us in his haste. But nothing was there. The creature was gone. He told me I must've dreamed it. But I know what I saw, and I know what it was. The Sasquatch come to take our souls."

"Interesting." Levesque glanced at Decker. "Now, why don't you tell us about your more recent encounter."

"Well, okay." Norwood hesitated a moment. His pale blue eyes glinted in the light from the fire. Then he began to talk again, and this time, no one else said a word.

TWELVE

"WHAT DO you make of Barry's story?" Decker stood near the tents with the zoologist, Theo Levesque, far enough from the campfire to be out of earshot, as long as he kept his voice low.

"Beats me." Levesque shrugged. "His father tells him a story about a Bigfoot, gets him all worked up, and then he sees one just like in the story. Years later, he comes back up here with his buddies and low and behold, another Bigfoot shows up."

"Hard to believe, isn't it?"

"It strains credibility for sure."

"Except that there were two other grown men up here with him. They all claimed to see it. The creature even attacked one of them. The man had to be carried out." Decker rubbed his chin. "Kind of makes you wonder."

"My money is still on a black bear. Those campfire tales his father liked to recite probably had him so terrified back then that he'd have claimed a squirrel was a Sasquatch. As for what happened up here last week . . . Well, he was telling the same story his father did before him. Look around you. It's nothing but creepy dark forest and open sky. We're miles from civilization. Easy for a person's imagination to run away with them in a place like this."

"Even so, three men . . ."

"I know."

"Two of whom didn't even believe Norwood's tale of giant hairy ape creatures running around the woods. All three reported the same experience."

"Look, I agree they had a run-in with something, okay? But it was dark, and they had Bigfoot on their minds. It's a case of mistaken identity, nothing more. A bear wanders past, gets curious, rises up on its hind legs. Bears can even walk upright for a spell. It's not the first time this has happened."

"Back to the bear theory again," Decker said, shaking his head.

"It's a valid hypothesis."

"Except most of those mistaken identity cases happen from afar. A glimpse of something walking in the forest. A dark shape higher up the mountain at dusk," Decker said. "In this instance, we have an intimate encounter. Three individuals who saw the same creature from as close as we are to that fire over there. One of them even grappled with the beast and came out on the losing end. Don't you think he would know if it was a bear?"

"You're forgetting one thing."

"What's that?" Decker asked.

"They were also in a state of merry inebriation. They admit they were drinking heavily. Drunk as skunks. I'm sure that if I'd been downing beers all day and night, and then met a garden variety bear in the dark forest, I might not recognize it for what it was either. I might even think it was a Bigfoot if

I was woozy enough and we'd been telling ghost stories to each other."

"Maybe you're right." Decker rubbed the bridge of his nose.

"That's what we came here to find out." Levesque glanced at his watch. "It's about time to turn in. A whole night sleeping under the stars. Maybe by tomorrow morning we'll have our answer."

"Maybe." Decker walked back to the campfire and stood staring into the flames. He hoped the Canadian zoologist was right, and it was just a trio of drunken men who tangled with an angry bear on a dark and cold fall night. But he couldn't shake the impression there was more to it than that. He felt like he was missing something, a nugget of information that danced tantalizingly out of reach at the back of his subconscious. He also felt a creeping sense of unease. A feeling that had come upon him as they walked up the narrow trail toward the campsite and had only grown in the hours of darkness since.

THIRTEEN

DECKER AWOKE to a dull thud against the side of his tent. He opened his eyes and looked at his watch. It was two in the morning.

He lay there listening, wondering if he had dreamed the sound. But then it came again. Whump. The side of his tent puckered in momentarily before springing back.

Decker slipped out of his sleeping bag and pulled his pants on, then crawled to the front of the tent and unzipped the flap. When he peeked out, he could see nothing except the glowing embers of the dying fire, the other tents, and the pitch-black forest beyond.

"John?" a voice drifted out of the darkness. "Is that you?"

"Yes." Decker recognized the voice as that of Theo Levesque. He scrambled out of the tent and stood up.

The Canadian was lingering next to one of the other tents, looking bewildered. "Did something hit the side of your tent, too?"

Decker nodded. "It woke me up."

"Me too. Which sucks because I was dreaming about . . .

Well, it doesn't matter." Levesque scratched his head. He wandered around to the side of the tent and bent down. When he straightened, there was a small round rock in his hand. "Come and look at this."

Decker joined him and saw several small rocks on the ground, then circled his own tent and found more of the smooth rocks. "Looks like someone has been having some fun with us."

"Why?" Levesque scratched his head. "And more to the point, who?"

"Beats me." Decker studied the tree line beyond the clearing, searching for any sign of an interloper.

"I can answer that."

Decker turned to see Barry Norwood standing near the remains of the fire with his arms folded. He was wearing a pair of thermal pajamas with a heavy hiking jacket over the top. Strand, fully dressed, stood behind him cradling the rifle and scanning their surroundings with keen interest.

Norwood stepped forward. "It isn't a who. It's more like a what."

"You mind sharing with us?" Decker said.

"It's the Bigfoot. That's what they do."

"Throw small stones at tents?" Levesque snorted. "Even if there were such a creature, why would they bother?"

"Protecting their territory. We're on their land." Barry rubbed his hands together against the cold and blew on them.

"Ridiculous." Levesque rolled his eyes.

"Maybe not," said Strand, his eyes still on the dark woods. "A couple of years ago, I accompanied an expedition that hiked into the wilderness of the Pacific Northwest to investigate a string of Sasquatch sightings. We didn't find anything, no one ever does, but two of the hunters who accompanied us claimed stones had been thrown at them the previous winter during an encounter." He looked at Decker. "This was before your time, which is why you weren't involved."

Decker said nothing, content to let the conversation run its course and listen.

Theo Levesque was not so restrained. "Of course you didn't find anything. And for the record, a few badly tossed rocks are hardly proof of a giant undiscovered cryptid with a bad attitude."

"Then how do you explain those?" Norwood said, nodding toward the discarded pebble-sized rocks lying between the tents. "Because they weren't there before."

"I'm sure there's a perfectly logical explanation." Levesque fixed Norwood with an icy stare. "Like someone playing a practical joke to prove their story. Hopefully, the trail cams captured something. When I retrieve the footage we might have our culprit."

"It wasn't me." Norwood's face turned an angry shade of red. "What, you think I cracked my best friend's skull and broke his ribs, too, just so I could say it was a Bigfoot?"

"You tell me."

"I wasn't the only one who saw the creature that night. We all did."

"And you were all more than a little intoxicated."

"Now look here—" Norwood took a step toward Levesque.

Strand placed himself between them and put a restraining hand on Norwood's chest. "That's enough. Both of you."

"He started it," Norwood said in a high-pitched voice.

"I don't care who's fault it was. This isn't the time or the place." Strand stared off into the forest. "We should check the perimeter, make sure nothing dangerous is skulking around out there. Does anyone else have a gun?"

"I do," said Decker. "Glock 19M. Used to be my backup weapon when I was a sheriff in Louisiana."

"Anyone else?"

Norwood shook his head.

Levesque glanced toward his tent. "Just the air rifle and tranq-darts. Non-lethal."

"Get it anyway." Strand turned his attention toward Decker. "I'll take Barry. You take Theo. We'll start off in opposite directions and circle the camp perimeter."

"Sounds reasonable." Decker ducked back into his tent as Strand and Norwood started toward the camp perimeter. He retrieved the gun from its hiding place in his backpack and turned it over in his palm. It was loaded, he knew, but he double-checked anyway, just to be sure. Then he exited the tent, straightened up, and made his way to Levesque, who was returning from his own tent with the air rifle slung over his shoulder. "Come on. Let's do this."

FOURTEEN

THEY FOLLOWED the perimeter of the campsite, skirting the woods but staying close to the safety of the small clearing where they had pitched their tents. Decker kept his gun at the low ready position, finger hovering on the frame above the trigger ready to slide down and fire should it become necessary, but he hoped it wouldn't.

Levesque kept pace at his shoulder, eyes darting around as if he expected some unknown creature to come crashing out of the woods at any moment, despite his professed skepticism. He carried a flashlight given to him by the Ghost Team operative, Strand, which he waved back and forth in slow arcs ahead of them to light their way.

The clearing within which they had made their camp took the shape of a rough oblong with the trail meandering through to one side and continuing on higher into the wilderness. Sugar maple, mountain ash, and poplar trees pressed in all directions around their campsite. With so much forest blanketing the State of Maine—ninety percent of the state was covered in woodland—Decker could easily believe that a reclusive primate had avoided all but the faintest contact with humanity since Europeans first set foot on this land hundreds of years before.

"You really think there's a Bigfoot up here?" Levesque asked in a half whisper as they moved around the back of the tents.

"Thought you didn't believe in this stuff." Decker threw a momentary glance toward the zoologist.

"Not sure if I do. But I've seen my share of weirdness since I came to work for CUSP, just like you." Levesque paused. "And your unofficial nickname around the water cooler wouldn't be *The Monster Hunter* without good cause."

"I told you already, I don't like that name. I don't hunt monsters," Decker hissed. Although even he had to admit that he'd run across more than a few of them, a fact that had whittled away at his own skepticism until he didn't know what was or wasn't real anymore. These days he found it as easy to believe in a Bigfoot as a goldfish. Although right now, he wasn't sure what to believe. That nagging feeling was back. The sense that he was missing something important. Again, it proved elusive, and he pushed it to the back of his mind.

Levesque shook his head. "This is a wild goose chase. There's nothing out here. I'm tired and cold and it's the middle of the night. I want to go back to the tent. We can search again in the morning. See if we can find any animal tracks . . . or maybe the boot prints of whoever threw those rocks."

"Still convinced we're being played, huh?" said Decker.

"Aren't you?"

"I don't know," Decker admitted. Up ahead he could see the beam of another flashlight, drawing closer to them. It was Strand and Norwood completing the circuit from the opposite direction. Given their relaxed gait, it didn't look like they had found anything, either.

This was confirmed a moment later when the pair drew close, and Strand raised an arm. "All clear on our end."

"Us too," Decker replied. "Didn't see or hear anything out of the ordinary."

"Well, something threw those rocks at the tents," Norwood said, glancing around nervously.

"Whatever it was, It's not here now."

"Which is fine by me." Levesque blew on his hands for warmth. "It's freezing out here and there's a toasty sleeping bag with my name on it back in the tent. I say we all go back to bed, and I'll look at the trail cams first thing in—"

He was interrupted by a warbling drawn-out howl.

"What the hell was that?" Levesque's head snapped sideways in the direction of the eerie noise. He slipped the air rifle off his shoulder.

"You tell us," Decker whispered. "You're the zoologist."

"I've never heard anything like it before." Levesque's face had drained of color.

"See. I told you," Norwood whispered, his voice cracking. "We're not alone out here."

"Quiet," snapped Strand. He turned to face the forest, raising his gun. "There's something moving out there. I can hear it."

Decker strained his ears to listen, and then he heard it too. A faint rustling, followed by the snap of a twig. There was definitely something moving in the darkness beyond the trees. Something big. And it was close.

FIFTEEN

"COME ON," said Decker to Strand. He took a step toward the forest where they had heard the strange howl. "Let's see what we're dealing with."

"Wait," Norwood said, his voice rising in panic. "You're not going to leave us here alone, are you?"

"Maybe we should come with you," Levesque said, although he didn't look keen to venture into the woods.

"No. The two of you should stay here." Decker shook his head. He glanced toward the fire pit and the glowing embers it contained. "Put more wood on the fire and stay close by. You should be safe."

"What if you don't come back?" Norwood didn't look convinced. "What if something happens to you?"

"Nothing's going to happen to us," Decker looked at Levesque. "Keep your air rifle handy. I know it only shoots tranqs, but if anything bigger than us comes at you out of those woods, use the rifle anyway."

"You can count on that," Levesque said. "Sure you don't want to take it?"

"I'm happy with what I've got." Strand patted his own, more lethal, weapon. "We get into a tangle I want stopping power."

"Keep the tranq-gun. You might need it." Decker took the flashlight from Levesque and then looked at Strand. "You ready?"

"Ready as I'll ever be." Strand clutched his rifle tight and started toward the woods.

Decker waited until the others had retreated to the safety of the fire pit and then followed along at a jog.

Once they left the clearing, darkness wrapped around them like a cloak. There was no sign of the moon. It was either too low on the horizon or shrouded by clouds.

The movement they had heard back at the camp had stopped now, making it hard to tell which direction they should go in. Decker made his best guess and pushed forward through the dense undergrowth that cloaked the forest floor, with Strand dropping back behind to cover their rear.

A chill breeze whipped up and blew through the forest, rustling leaves and making Decker wish he'd taken the time to put on a coat.

They moved slowly and on high alert, listening for any sign of whatever had thrown rocks at the tents. Decker swung the flashlight's beam around, searching the dark spaces between tree trunks. A couple of times, he lifted the flashlight and shone it higher, just in case something was lurking overhead in the canopy. But the further they got from camp, the more Decker believed that whatever had made that howl had moved off and was no longer in the area. It was possible their own intrusion into the forest had scared it away.

He came to a halt near a fallen tree and scanned their

surroundings before turning to Strand. "What do you think?" He asked in a voice barely above a whisper.

"I think that whatever we heard has called it a night," Strand replied. "We might as well head back."

"I was thinking the same thing." Decker didn't want to leave the others alone for any longer than necessary. He didn't believe they were in any real danger, and Levesque had the air rifle, but he didn't want to take the chance. He started back in the direction of the clearing. But then, before he'd even made it ten feet, there was a quick rustling of leaves off to their left.

Strand froze. "You hear that?"

Decker nodded and turned in the direction of the sound. He motioned for Strand to follow and moved toward it with all the stealth he could muster.

Then he noticed something else. A woodsy, musty odor, unlike anything he'd smelled before. It assaulted his nostrils and burned at the back of his throat. One glance toward Strand confirmed that the Ghost Team operative had noticed it, too.

"What on earth is that stench?" Strand muttered under his breath. "It's foul."

Decker didn't answer. Instead, he lifted a finger to his lips and stopped, because a pair of eyes were looking back at them from the underbrush dead ahead. A pair of eyes that blinked once, twice, three times. Then they were gone just as quickly as they had appeared, melting back into the forest darkness.

The hairs on the back of Decker's neck stood up. He held his breath.

Strand raised his rifle.

The Glock was a reassuring weight in Decker's hand. He swung the flashlight in a wide arc to illuminate the patch of foliage where the eyes had been, but nothing was there now. Just a tangle of branches and a scraggly shrub. Lower down, wild sarsaparilla spread across the ground in a leafy green carpet.

Decker lowered the flashlight and stood listening. At first there was nothing, but then he picked up the sound of movement off to their right. He glanced at Strand. "Hear that?"

The Ghost Team operative nodded. "Whatever's out here is circling us."

"I was afraid you'd say that." Decker brought the flashlight back up. "The question is what do—"

Before he could finish, the understory parted, and a dark shape lunged toward them.

SIXTEEN

DECKER STAGGERED BACKWARD, caught off guard. His heel struck a half-buried rock and then he pitched backward. As he fell, Decker caught a glimpse of Strand, leaping sideways to avoid whatever had sprung at them. Then he hit the ground hard, knocking the wind out of him. The Glock jarred loose from his grip and landed a few feet away.

There was a flash of movement. A sense of something large and hairy. Powerful. Decker caught a whiff of that same noxious odor carried on the breeze as the creature passed by.

A rifle cracked, the single gunshot echoing around the forest and reverberating back.

From somewhere off in the darkness, Strand cursed. "I missed."

Decker hauled himself to his feet. He scooped up the pistol and gave chase, ignoring the barbs and branches that caught at his clothes and raked his arms and face. He shone the flashlight forward—caught glimpses of the creature as it smashed through the woods at a breakneck pace. It ran upright on two legs, at least seven feet tall, and was definitely not a bear.

Strand had joined the pursuit. Decker could hear him following along behind, but he didn't dare glance back for fear of losing the creature in the dense forest.

But that was exactly what happened.

He caught one final peek of the beast as it passed between two fat tree trunks, and then, without warning, lost it for good.

When he reached the spot where he last saw the beast, Decker pulled up short. There was no sign of the creature. The malodorous scent was gone, too. Decker didn't understand how, but the hulking, enormous creature had escaped their pursuit. Vanished into thin air.

He looked around in disbelief, chest heaving. From somewhere off to his left, came the sound of water. A gurgling tinkle in the darkness. There must be a stream cutting through the forest somewhere nearby.

"Where did it go?" Strand asked, catching up with him. The man looked about as winded as Decker felt. A trickle of blood ran down his cheek where a thorny branch had snagged him.

"Damned if I know." Decker's lungs burned. He felt a stitch needling his side. "Don't ask me how, but it got away."

SEVENTEEN

WHEN THEY RETURNED to the campsite, Levesque and Norwood had the fire going again and were now huddled near the crackling flames.

Norwood clutched a small silver canteen, which he sipped at intervals. As they approached, he stood up. "We heard a gunshot. Are you both okay?"

"We're fine." Decker looked at the canteen. "Took a potshot at whatever was out there."

"Purely in self-defense," said Strand. "Not that it did any good. Damned thing was moving mighty fast, and I was half-blind. No moon tonight. Missed by a mile."

"Shame." Norwood held out the flask. "Want a nip?"

"That's not water, just so you know," Levesque said in a mildly disapproving tone.

"Bourbon." Norwood took another sip and smacked his lips. "Helps calm the nerves."

"You sure that's a good idea?" Decker asked, casting a wary eye toward the forest lest the creature return. "We need to keep our wits about us."

"Lighten up, pops." Norwood scowled. "I can handle my whisky."

Pops? Decker raised an eyebrow. Norwood was about the same age as him. "Whatever. You're a grown man."

"Thank you." Norwood's scowl slipped away. His gaze shifted to the forest. "Did you see it?"

"We saw *something* . . . we gave chase when it took off." Strand glanced back toward the forest. "We were gaining on it, too, would have caught it, except the damned thing vanished from right under our noses."

"For the record, you were right. It's not a bear," Decker said. "And it's not very friendly either."

"Not that we got a long look at it," said Strand. "Just a few quick glimpses when it charged us. It's pretty dark out there. Hard to see much beyond our own noses, even with the flashlights."

"It attacked you?"

"I'm not sure it was attacking so much as trying to scare us away," Decker said. "A warning shot across our bows, so to speak. If it really wanted to hurt us, it could have. The thing was at least seven feet tall and must have weighed four hundred pounds."

"See? Now do you believe there's a Bigfoot out here?" Norwood said, his gaze shifting to Levesque.

"I believe there's something roaming these woods, but a few animal noises and second-hand accounts aren't enough to convince me it's a Bigfoot."

"Unbelievable." Norwood shook his head. "You won't accept the evidence even when it's right in front of you."

"Look, I agree with Mr. Decker. It's probably not a bear. But that doesn't prove we're dealing with a hitherto unknown species of hominid that's evaded discovery for hundreds of years."

"What *do you* think it is, then?" Norwood asked.

"Right now, all I'm willing to admit is that there's clearly a large and powerful animal roaming around this forest. An exotic pet of some kind that got loose. A big cat or maybe a chimpanzee."

"That's a ridiculous idea."

"Is it?" Levesque folded his arms. "Makes more sense than Sasquatch."

"It wasn't a big cat. You call yourself a zoologist?" Norwood snorted. "How about you, Mr. Decker? You think it's an exotic pet?"

"No. It wasn't a big cat or anything like that." Decker shook his head. "I can't think of any exotic pet that would walk on two legs like this did. But I couldn't say it's a Bigfoot either. I don't have an explanation for what we saw. Not yet."

"Good enough for me." Norwood put the flask to his lips and tilted it back. A look of disappointment came over him. "Think I need a refill."

"I think you've had enough for one night." Decker stepped forward and took the flask from his hand.

"Hey." Norwood made a flailing grab for it.

Decker sidestepped the clumsy attempt. "You can have the flask back tomorrow when you've sobered up. If that creature returns and we need to leave in a hurry, I don't want to end up carrying you out of here."

Norwood shrugged. "No worries. I've got a bottle in the tent, anyway."

"Not anymore, you don't." Strand turned toward Norwood's tent. He bent low and crawled inside, coming out a moment later with a half-full bottle of bourbon. He removed the cap and poured it out over the fire, watching the flames leap higher as they consumed the alcohol. "Problem solved."

Norwood glared at him but said nothing.

Decker glanced at his watch. "It won't be daylight for several hours. I suggest we return to our tents and try to get some sleep. Tomorrow we'll take a look around, see if we can find any evidence of what we encountered in the woods tonight."

"Don't forget the trail cams," Levesque said. "I'll retrieve the memory cards in the morning and see if anything activated them."

Decker nodded.

"I'll stay out here by the fire if it's all the same with you," Strand said. "Someone should remain awake and keep guard in case our nocturnal visitor returns."

"Good idea," Decker said. "You can keep watch for a couple of hours, then wake me and I'll take over. You need rest, too."

Strand nodded. "It's almost three A.M. I'll wake you at five-thirty."

"Sounds like a plan." Decker looked at Norwood and Levesque. "Now, everyone back to your tents."

EIGHTEEN

DECKER HARDLY SLEPT despite his own advice and lay staring at the sides of the tent until it was his turn to keep watch. He exited the tent before Strand even had time to fetch him, and approached the firepit, where the Ghost Team operative was sitting in a camping chair with the rifle leaning next to him.

Strand looked up at his approach. "You're ten minutes early."

"Couldn't sleep."

"Yeah. I get that."

"Any movement since our encounter in the forest?" Decker asked.

"Nothing." Strand stood and shook his head. He offered the rifle to Decker. "Here's hoping it stays that way."

"Roger that." The rifle felt heavy in Decker's hands. Much better than the Glock, which he now offered up in its place.

Strand took the proffered weapon with a nod. "Thanks."

"I want that back later," Decker said. It held sentimental

value for him as one of the few remaining connections to his former life as a sheriff in Wolf Haven, Louisiana. Nancy was the other connection. An old high school sweetheart with whom he'd reconnected with upon returning there after many years in New York as a homicide detective. Now she was his fiancée.

"Like I'm going to let you keep the rifle." Strand grinned and started toward his tent. "I'm going to hit the sack for a few hours. Wake me when it's time for breakfast."

Decker watched him leave, then settled into a chair next to the fire. He threw another log on and looked out at the brooding, empty forest. Somewhere in that vast wilderness was an unknown creature. Perhaps it was many miles away by now, or maybe it was somewhere in the dense foliage looking back at him. That thought made Decker shudder, and he pushed it from his mind, trying to think of something else. Anything else. But over and over, his thoughts returned to the creature they had encountered out in the woods. Something wasn't right about the situation, but still, he could not put his finger on it.

An hour and a half went by.

The sun began its slow ascent, peeking above the top of the trees and throwing long golden rays across the fall landscape.

He threw another log on the fire then settled back in the chair and watched the trees at the edge of the clearing, and the gloomy spaces between. Nothing stirred. He yawned.

"What, no breakfast yet? I'm starving."

Decker looked around to see Strand walking toward him. "You know I'm not the camp cook, right? Besides, the others aren't up yet."

"You could at least have put a pot of coffee on," Strand said, looking at the stainless-steel quart-sized coffee percolator sitting next to the circle of stones they had gathered to surround the campfire the previous day.

"I can fix that right now." Decker reached for the percolator. "Want to take a look around after breakfast? See what we can find."

"Sure."

"Count me in, too," said a voice from behind them. Levesque was striding toward them from the direction of his tent. He was dressed in khaki pants and a cable-knit sweater. When he reached Decker and Strand, he came to a halt and dug his hands into his pockets.

"The ground is soft right now. Whatever was out there last night must have left tracks. Find those, and we can identify whatever was skulking around our camp last night. I'd also like to pull the memory cards from the trail cams and see what they caught, if anything." Levesque glanced toward the forest. "Then maybe we can put this matter to rest and get back to civilization."

NINETEEN

EVEN IN DAYLIGHT, the woods were tough going. The trees were packed tightly together amid a tangle of dense understory. Boulders large and small heaved from the ground. And then there was the poison ivy, with vines creeping up tree trunks and spreading across the ground as an itchy, unpleasant shrub. Decker did his best to avoid the plant's distinctive three-pointed leaves and hairy vines, but it wasn't easy, and he was soon glad for his sturdy hiking boots, thick socks, and denim jeans.

"How are we ever going to find anything out here?" Norwood said, trailing a few feet behind the others. "It's like a needle in a haystack."

"If something was here last night, we'll find proof of it," replied Levesque. He was carrying a small green backpack slung over one shoulder. Inside were the tools of his trade. Field notebook made with all-weather paper, multi-tool camping knife, compass, and a small digital camera. He also carried glass jars and tweezers for collecting specimens. A pair of binoculars hung around his neck. He looked every bit the field scientist.

"We know something was here," Decker said. "Because we saw it with our own eyes. Chased it."

"I don't suppose you could lead us to the spot where you had your encounter?" Levesque asked hopefully.

"We can try," Strand replied. "It was pitch black out here last night. We could barely see anything, even with the flashlights."

Decker nodded. "And it all looks different in the cold light of day."

Strand slowed and looked around. "I remember hearing a stream last night after we lost the creature. Maybe we should see if we can find it again."

"Streams are a great place to look for tracks," Levesque said. "Animals need water, so you can bet that anything living in this forest is visiting the stream."

"It can't be far from here." Decker brought the small group to a halt and motioned for them to be quiet.

They listened in silence, trying to pick out the gurgle of running water from the general background noise of the forest.

After half a minute, Decker shook his head. "I don't hear it."

"Me either." Strand stood with his hands resting on his hips. He turned a full three-sixty, scanning the woods.

"I think it was this way," Decker said, although he was far from sure. He took the lead, pushing deeper into the forest. After a couple of minutes, they heard the unmistakable sound of running water. Soon a small brook appeared ahead of them, cascading down through the landscape and dropping over boulders in miniature waterfalls.

"This is it." Strand came to a halt near the brook. "The

creature went in this direction before we lost it. Tread carefully so we don't destroy any trace evidence it left behind."

"I don't see anything." Norwood was studying their surroundings.

"It won't be obvious." Levesque motioned for the others to stay where they were and took a couple of steps toward the stream, studying his surroundings as he went. After a few minutes, he let out an exclamation. "Found something. Look here."

Decker and the others hurried forward.

Levesque was already slipping the pack off his shoulder. He unzipped it and removed a small glass vial and a pair of tweezers. He handed them to Decker. "Hold these a moment."

"What is it?" Decker asked.

"Organic matter." Levesque reached for the digital camera now. He snapped a couple of photographs, leaning close to a bush that hugged the water's edge.

"What does that mean?" Norwood asked, peering around Decker and Strand. "Organic matter?"

"Hair." Levesque put the camera away and took back the items he had given to Decker. He unscrewed the metal lid from the glass vial and reached toward the bush with the tweezers. "The branches in this spot snagged on an animal as it passed by. Judging from the height of the branch, it must have been big. With any luck, it's the same creature we were chasing in the woods last night."

Decker watched as the zoologist plucked a knot of wiry black hair off the branch.

"Can you identify what animal the hair came from?" Norwood asked.

"Not out here." Levesque shook his head. He dropped it

into the vial and screwed the lid back on. "I'll need access to a lab for that. We'll have to run a DNA sequence."

"And compare it to known species." Strand was staring at the vial with keen interest. "Just like with the earlier sample."

"Precisely. And if it doesn't match any known animal in the database, that will be an answer in itself."

Norwood watched as Levesque tucked the vial back into his backpack. "But you won't be able to tell if it's a Bigfoot?"

"Correct. Since no one has ever found one and entered the creature's genetic makeup into a database, the best we can hope for is to find Simian DNA, from which we could conclude that it came from an unknown primate."

"How long will that take?"

"Weeks. Maybe a month or more." Levesque was looking down at the stream. Now he made another exclamation. His eyes flew wide. "We have more evidence."

Decker followed his gaze and saw what had excited the zoologist. There, visible in a patch of muddy soil next to the stream, was a wide footprint with the clear impression of an arched heel and four fat toes.

TWENTY

"THERE'S YOUR PROOF OF A BIGFOOT," Norwood said, his voice rising a few notes. His eyes were wide with excitement. "I told you it was real."

"One solitary footprint proves nothing," Levesque replied. "See how wet the mud is? Just because the print looks big now doesn't mean it started out that way. The mud might have flattened out and settled to make it look bigger."

"Then tell me what type of animal has four toes like that." Norwood wasn't giving up.

"Again, what looks like toes could be the eroded impressions of claws."

"You think this was a black bear?" Strand asked him, bending to get a better look at the print.

Levesque shook his head. "As it happens, I don't. Even if the footprint has spread out and flattened, it's the wrong shape. But I'm not quite at the point where I would declare it a Bigfoot impression either. At best, it's unidentified."

"Which leaves us no better off than we were before," grumbled Norwood. "What's the point of looking for evidence if you won't believe your own eyes when you find it?"

"The point is to prove we are dealing with a real animal and not just a bunch of overactive imaginations." Levesque sounded irritated.

"It wasn't a figment of my imagination that came charging at us in the woods last night," Strand said. "We're dealing with a real animal, all right."

"I agree." Levesque nodded. He removed a small wooden ruler from his pack and placed it next to the footprint, then took another series of photographs. "The best thing we can do is record our findings for further study. Maybe when we get the hair samples back, we'll know more."

"Shouldn't we make a plaster cast of that footprint?" Strand asked.

"We could if we had any quick-drying plaster."

"But we don't, huh?"

"Nope."

"Guess we'll have to make do with the photos, then." Strand looked around. "If the creature crossed the stream right here, there could be more footprints on the other bank."

"Worth taking look." Decker was already crossing the water, stepping from rock to rock to avoid getting his boots wet.

Levesque followed, after telling the others to stay right where they were. Too many sets of feet might obliterate any remaining evidence.

But when he examined the ground, Decker was disappointed to find nothing of interest. If the creature had crossed the stream here, it had left no further evidence of its passage.

"Shame," said Levesque, as if reading Decker's mind. "If we found more prints, it might give us a better idea what animal left them, what its stride length was, and if it was bipedal."

"You want to keep going?" Decker asked, staring off into the forest.

Levesque shook his head. "I can't see the point. We're not even sure the creature actually crossed the stream here, but if it did, we don't know in which direction it went after that. There's a lot of dense forest up here. Tens of thousands of square miles. The chances of coming across anything else are slim. I'd like to collect the memory cards from the trail cams and see if they caught anything. There's one not far from here. Maybe we'll get lucky."

"Sounds like a plan." Decker started back across the stream to rejoin the rest of the group. He cast one last glance down toward the faint indentation in the mud where the creature had walked the previous night, then he let Levesque take them to the first trail cam, which was positioned several hundred feet from the stream on a maple tree.

The zoologist removed the memory card and slipped a new one in, then reset the camera before moving off through the forest, circling the clearing until they came to a second camera where he repeated the procedure. They moved on to the third camera, then the fourth, located near the trail. Finally, with all the memory cards safely in his pocket, Levesque turned back toward camp. But when they emerged from the forest, he came to a sudden halt.

Decker, trailing a few paces behind, almost walked into his back. At first, he wasn't sure why the zoologist had stopped short, but when he looked past him toward their camp, he understood.

TWENTY-ONE

"WHAT THE HELL?" Levesque pushed past Strand and ran into the clearing, looking around in horror. "Who could have done this?"

"That's a good question," Decker said, stepping into the clearing and looking around at the wrecked camp site.

The fire pit they had constructed the afternoon before and tended through the night had been trampled, partially burned logs and ash kicked beyond the ring of stones. Their chairs were upended. One was clear across the campsite and now lay on its back near the trees. The tents had fared no better. All four had collapsed, or more likely, deliberately flattened. The pegs holding them down had been ripped from the ground. But that was not all. The contents of their backpacks were strewn across the clearing, along with their provisions. Bottled water, cans of food, protein bars, fruit. It was a mess.

"Looks like a tornado came through here," Strand said, joining Decker.

"Not a tornado." Norwood's voice cracked. "Bigfoot. It

must have come into camp while we were out in the woods."

"Or a moose," Strand said. "We should eliminate all other possibilities before jumping to conclusions."

"A moose didn't do this." Levesque shook his head. "Rutting season is over, and even then, a moose would be unlikely to rampage through a campsite like this for no good reason. I'd say a bear wandered in looking for food before heading into its den for the winter, but apart from being scattered around the place, none of the food has been touched."

"We were never that far away from the camp, and we didn't hear a thing." Decker crossed to his collapsed tent and picked up some discarded clothing, which he draped over his arm. "Whatever came in here was quick and quiet."

"And angry," Strand added. "My money's on whatever the hell we were chasing in the woods last night."

"Right." Decker picked up his rucksack and began putting his clothes and other belongings back inside. "Which leads us right back to a creature of unknown origin inhabiting these woods."

"Bigfoot," Norwood said, reiterating his earlier claim.

Decker shrugged. "I guess it doesn't matter what we call it, the damage is done. We appear to have wandered into the habitat of something that does not want us here."

Strand was inspecting the tents. "Well, it's going to be stuck with us for a while longer. The camp is a hell of a mess, but nothing seems to be damaged beyond repair. We'll have the tents back up in under an hour and the rest of this stuff cleaned up in two."

"Or we could just pack up and hike back out of here," Norwood said, glancing nervously toward the forest. "Haven't you seen enough?"

"We haven't even gotten started yet," Decker said.

"What about the trail cam footage?" Norwood glanced toward Levesque.

"I was going to go through the memory cards just as soon as we got back to camp," Levesque said, walking over to the remains of his tent. "Of course, that was before we discovered the place ransacked."

"Even more reason to go back." Norwood watched Levesque pluck his laptop from beneath the folds of the collapsed tent. "I didn't sign up for this."

"We are all here because of you," Strand said. He looked at Levesque. "Is the laptop damaged?"

"Give me a minute, and I'll tell you." The zoologist opened it and pressed the power button. After a minute, the screen lit up. "I had it turned off to preserve the battery. Looks like it's fine, thank goodness."

"That's one thing, at least." Strand pushed his hands into his pockets. "Your priority is to look at those memory cards and see if they caught anything out of the ordinary. The rest of us will clean the campsite and put the tents back up."

Levesque nodded and made his way across the campsite to a fallen tree trunk near the edge of the clearing. He sat down on it and got to work, ignoring the others as they went about putting the campsite to rights.

After an hour, the tents were standing again with everyone's personal items stashed safely within, and the scattered provisions were back where they belonged. Strand had built a fire which now crackled in the center of the clearing. That done, he set about making a late lunch of canned stew cooked over the open flames.

By the time it was ready, Levesque had finished going through the images on the memory cards. He approached the group with a somber expression. "The trail cams recorded nothing out of the ordinary. Just the occasional deer wandering by, a few birds, and a coyote that made a brief cameo before wandering off. A few unidentifiable photos that could be anything. Unfortunately, whatever we encountered last night did a good job of steering clear."

"How is that possible?" Norwood asked, accepting a bowl of stew from Strand. He scooped some with his spoon and blew on it. "We all heard it."

Levesque shrugged. "I only have four cameras. Nowhere near enough to capture everything that's walking around out here. Even a hundred cameras couldn't do that. There's a lot of terrain and it's so densely wooded. It was always a long shot. Honestly, even if we got a photograph of whatever is out there, there's no guarantee we'd be able to identify it. There are so many variables in capturing images of animals at night—light balance, shutter speed, distance from the camera, how fast the subject is moving—that we might very well end up with nothing but a blur. Especially if our subject is too close to the camera."

"You're saying the trail cams are useless." Norwood frowned.

"No. I'm just saying that we can't expect miracles." Levesque glanced toward the trees. "It might be worth moving a camera closer to that stream we found. If something is crossing there, we'll have a better chance of getting a look at it."

"Good idea," said Strand. "We'll do it as soon as we finish eating."

"Not all of us," said Decker. "I don't think we should leave the camp unattended again."

"I agree." Strand dipped his spoon into the stew. "From now on, someone always stays close by and alert. Night or day, we don't let our guard down. This time, it was just our tents that got flattened. Next time, it might be one of us."

TWENTY-TWO

ADDIE WELLS SLOGGED up the trail with a scowl on her face. It was early evening and already getting dark. Even though they were close to their destination, they still had to set up the campsite when they got there. They should have left at dawn for the three hour drive up into northern Maine and equally long trek on foot into the wilderness once they had gone as far as the car would take them. But after their late-night adventure, neither she nor Cam had possessed the will to climb out of bed while it was still dark. Now, though, she was regretting her earlier laziness.

"How much further is it?" She asked, stepping around a large boulder that protruded into the trail and hurrying to catch up with Cam who was several steps ahead.

"Maybe another half mile."

Addie groaned. Her feet hurt, and she was cold despite the heavy winter jacket, gloves, and woolen hat she wore. The trail was tough going, too, and more than once she had tripped on an exposed root despite the LED headlamp she wore over her hat that lit their way in the gloomy darkness under the tree canopy. "Maybe we should just stop here and make camp, then hike up to the site tomorrow morning."

"No. I want to get there tonight." Cam could be stubborn at times, and this was one of them.

"You owe me for this." Addie hadn't even wanted to come out into the wilderness. She thought Cam was being ridiculous, not to mention a little underhanded in the way he was treating Professor Calloway, a man he professed to admire. But she also loved him, so here she was. "You owe me big time."

"And I'll repay you ten times over when we're finished up here," Cam said, repeating the promise he'd made several times over the last few days. "I appreciate your support. Really, I do."

"Yeah, well, my support is reaching its limit. Especially after you made me break into the professor's office last night."

"You won't be complaining when we find what we came here for." Cam stopped and waited a moment to let her finally catch up and draw level with him. He put an arm around her shoulder. "It will all be worth it."

"It had better be." Addie shrugged his arm away and started off again. "We could be eating brick oven pizza at Franco's right now instead of trudging up this trail into the middle of nowhere."

"You can have all the pizza you want when we get back." Cam rounded a corner on the trail and came to a sudden halt.

Addie, who wasn't expecting him to stop, took a few more steps, then turned back in surprise. "What are you doing?"

"Hush." Cam waved an arm to silence her. "I thought I heard something. Voices."

Addie looked around and strained to listen, but the

surrounding forest was quiet. She laughed nervously. "You're hearing things."

"I wasn't hearing things." Cam whispered before falling silent and standing on the trail like a statue.

Addie folded her arms and waited. Still, she heard nothing beyond the normal sounds of the forest. Rustling leaves. The occasional bird chirping high in the branches. She was about to say they should keep going, that he was being paranoid, when another sound filtered through the undergrowth.

Voices. At least two of them. Both men.

Cam was right. Someone else was out here with them.

"I think it's coming from up ahead on the trail," Cam said in the same low voice. He started forward again, moving more cautiously now.

Addie followed behind, trying not to make any noise that would give them away. Which was ridiculous, because they were on public land, and it wasn't unusual to come across other hikers out on the trails. Except that most people didn't hike in the winter, and the events of the previous twenty-four hours, breaking into the professor's office, coming up here to steal the fruits of his research out from under him, had left her paranoid. On edge.

Cam rounded another corner, then he stepped quickly off the trail and crouched down behind a tangle of bushes and looked over the top before pulling his head down again. When Addie kneeled next to him, he turned to her. "There are a bunch of guys around a campfire up ahead. We aren't alone."

Addie risked a peek and saw that he was right. There was a clearing with a camp set up not far ahead of them. In the middle of the camp sat four men around a roaring fire. They were deep in conversation. She turned to Cam. "Why do you think they're here?"

"Beats me." Cam shrugged. "But it's a mighty coincidence that they just happen to be so close to where we're going, especially at this time of year."

"You think they work for Professor Calloway?"

"Maybe. They could be here for the same reason as us. Or maybe they're just a bunch of guys who came up here for some peace and quiet. There's only one way to find out."

"What's that?" Addie had a feeling she would not like the answer.

Cam stood up and started back toward the trail. "We stroll in there and introduce ourselves. Act like we're just up here for a spot of winter camping."

"You think they'll buy that?" Addie joined him.

"That depends. If they really are just here by coincidence, then they won't give us a second thought. But if they're here following McAllister's clues, then we have a problem."

"And how are we going to know one way or the other?"

Cam shrugged again. "I guess we'll just have to see how they react when we show up. Come on." He beckoned for her to follow him up the trail. "Let's get this over with. And try to act natural. Friendly. Understood?"

"Sure." Addie pushed her hands into her pockets and followed Cam. A moment later, the camp came into view.

TWENTY-THREE

DECKER and the rest of his small group were sitting around the campfire discussing the harrowing events of the previous twenty-four hours when a movement further down the trail caught his eye. Beams of light that bobbed through the trees.

Soon after, two figures came into view, hiking toward them. A man and a woman, both in their early twenties. He was tall and lean, with short-cropped dark hair. She was slim and athletic, with a cascade of dark blond locks that fell around her shoulders. Both wore thick jackets, woolen hats, and gloves. Heavy backpacks were slung over their shoulders. The light had come from bright LED headlamps each hiker wore to illuminate their way on the dark trail. The young man held a small yellow GPS navigator unit— probably because cell phones didn't work so far from civilization rendering the maps feature useless. They both carried powerful flashlights that they swept across the ground ahead of them.

As they approached, the man slid the GPS navigator into

his pocket and raised a hand in greeting.

"Hiya fellow wanderers." The man was grinning. "Don't mind us. We're just passing through. We'll be on our way a little further up the trail before you know it."

"Sorry to come barging in on your campsite while you're finishing supper," said the young woman.

"Think nothing of it," said Decker, standing to greet them as they drew close.

"Name's Cam. Short for Cameron," said the man. He motioned toward his companion. "This is Addie."

"Pleased to meet you." Addie held up a hand in greeting.

"John." Decker glanced back over his shoulder toward the others, who were still sitting around the campfire. He introduced them. Each man waved in turn.

"Hiya," Cam said again. He reached up and turned off his headlamp. "We're planning on staking our claim a little further up the trail. Do a little winter camping. There's a cozy spot I found last time I was here. It's about a quarter mile away. We'll only be around a couple of nights. So, what are you guys doing up here?"

"Camping, same as you," Strand replied without elaborating. "Speaking of which, you're out on the trail a bit late, aren't you? I wouldn't want to be night hiking out here."

Cam shrugged. "Yeah. It's a hell of a trek here from the trailhead and we got caught in traffic after we left Bangor. Got here later than we would have liked. But it's fine. We know the area. We'll build a fire as soon as we get to camp and have the tent up in a jiffy."

"No biggie," Addie said with a grin. "We'll stick close to the trail."

"Maybe you should camp here with us," Strand said. "There's plenty of room and safety in numbers."

"We appreciate the offer," Cam rubbed his hands together. "But we'll press on, our campsite isn't too far."

Addie didn't look convinced. "What do you mean, safety in numbers?"

"We encountered something last night," Strand said. "An unidentified animal. Something big."

From behind them, Norwood piped up. "It's not unidentified. It was a Bigfoot."

"I'm sorry?" A flash of disbelief passed across Cam's face. "Did you say Bigfoot?"

"We don't know that for sure." Strand looked back over his shoulder with a scowl. "You'll have to ignore our friend. He has an overactive imagination."

"Now look here . . ." Norwood jumped up. "You can't deny what happened last night. We were attacked."

"Attacked?" The confidence had vanished from Cam's voice.

Norwood stepped closer to the two hikers. "Something threw rocks at our tents. When we went to investigate it charged at us."

"You mean like it came into your camp?" Addie glanced around, nervous.

"No." Decker shook his head. "We came across an animal out in the forest while we were looking for whatever threw the stones at us. We spooked it."

"I don't like this." Addie took a step closer to Cam. She gripped his arm. "Maybe we should turn around. Go back down."

"Do you think it's still around?" Cam asked. "Is the animal dangerous?"

"I don't know," Decker said. "But I wouldn't advise hiking back down the trail in the dark. Much too treacherous. Even if you don't run across a bear or some other angry critter, you could trip and break a leg."

"I agree," said Strand. "There are stream-cut ravines all around these parts. Loose rocks and boulders."

"And you don't want to stray off the trail in the darkness and get yourselves lost," Decker added. "My colleague is right. You should camp here with us tonight."

"That might be for the best," Addie said.

"No way." Cam shook his head. "It was probably just a bear. So long as we stick close to the trail, keep the fire burning, and don't venture out of camp, we'll be just fine. And if we need help it's not far away."

"Cam . . ." Addie's eyes were wide. "Listen to what these people are trying to tell you."

"They said it might not even be in the area anymore." Cam was having none of it.

"That's not exactly what I said." Decker wondered if the young man was being stubborn to impress his girlfriend. False bravado. He also wondered if Cam thought that staying with Decker and the others would cramp his style. It was hard to fool around when you were so close to four other tents inhabited by strangers.

"Do you have a gun?" Strand asked. "Anything to defend yourselves with?"

"I have this," Addie said, slipping the pack off her back and unzipping it. She pulled out a small can of pepper spray.

Strand made a huffing sound. "Hate to tell you this, but if you were hoping to use that on anything bigger than a squirrel, you're out of luck."

"You need bear spray," said Decker.

"Oh. Really?" Addie looked surprised. "My self-defense instructor in college told us this was a must."

"Against some creep following you home from the bar at midnight," Strand said. "Not so great against a five hundred pound wild animal that thinks you got too close to its cubs."

"Come on, Addie." Cam adjusted the pack on his shoulders. "We're perfectly safe. I read up online before we left to come up here. Even if we do run across a black bear, they're pretty docile most of the time. They'll just walk in the other direction. We have nothing to worry about."

"That's true," Strand said. "But the creature we encountered last night might not be a black bear."

"Oh, right. Sasquatch." Cam laughed and shook his head. "We'll be sure to keep our eyes peeled and hey, if we do come across it I'll take a few photos and we'll be famous!"

"Cam. Don't joke." Addie cast a worried glance toward her boyfriend. "I really think—"

Cam cut her off. "We're camping up at the ridge just like we planned. Grab your pack and let's go before we lose the last of the light." He turned his attention to Decker and Strand. "Thanks for the warning."

"Our pleasure," Decker said.

"If you change your minds or need help, we'll be here." Strand folded his arms.

"We appreciate that," Cam said as they started off across the clearing toward the trail on the other side.

Addie cast a glance over her shoulder and smiled. "Have a good evening."

"You, too." Decker watched them leave with a sense of foreboding. He would have preferred they make camp in the clearing and not venture deeper into the forest. He turned to Strand. "Think they'll be okay?"

Strand turned back to the fire. "I hope so."

TWENTY-FOUR

AS SOON AS they were further up the trail and out of earshot, Addie turned to Cam. "What do you think they're doing up here?

"How would I know?" Cam glanced back over his shoulder.

"You don't think they're up here for the same reason as us, do you? All that talk about some kind of wild animal on the loose. A Bigfoot. It was like they were trying to scare us away."

"Yeah, well, it isn't going to work. And if they are up here to find the stash, they're going to be disappointed. For a start, they're camping in the wrong place."

Addie felt a sudden hang of apprehension. "What if they were telling the truth?"

"About Bigfoot roaming around?" Cam laughed. "Give me a freaking break."

"I think we should be careful, anyway." Addie bit her bottom lip.

Cam stopped on the trail and turned to her. He took her

hand. "Look, I've been up in these woods at least three times with Professor Calloway and the rest of the research team. If there was anything out here, we would have seen it. Besides, there's no such thing as Bigfoot."

"You're right, of course." Addie nodded.

They started back up the trail in silence. It was dark and she wondered if Cam would recognize their destination when he saw it. He might have come up here before with the professor, but they were in an entirely different location a couple of miles from the site where the research team had been working. He'd never actually been to this particular spot. But then, just when she thought they were lost, he let out a whoop and waved the GPS tracker in front of her.

"This is the spot. We're here." Cam stepped off the trail and slid his backpack off, placing it on the ground in a flat area between the trees.

"You sure?" Addie looked around. It didn't look like much. Just more woodland.

"I'm sure. I worked it out the last time the professor brought us up here, and I double checked it before we left against Captain McAllister's papers. That's why we had to break into the professor's office last night. I didn't want to forget something and end up at wrong place."

"If you say so." Addie was already regretting this trip. As far as she was concerned, it was a fool's errand. Professor Calloway had filled Cam's head with tall tales. She had no doubt the Revolutionary war era British captain had been out in these woods—after all, the professor had found evidence of his presence at the location where his regiment were rumored to have made camp on their way north—but she didn't believe the legends about the rest of it for a second. "I don't understand. Why would McAllister come all the way here when his camp was at least a mile away?"

"We've been through this," Cam said with a sigh. "In December 1775, the Continental Army was pushing up into Maine—which was part of Massachusetts back then—for the Invasion of Québec. Days before, McAllister and his men had raided a small town looking for provisions on their way to British controlled Québec City. But he took much more than food and drink. He stole a chest of cash, mostly coinage, from the townsfolk. Money they needed to live. The Continental Army were closing in and McAllister was afraid they would catch up with him before he reached safety. If that happened, he didn't want the proof of his crime close at hand. He came out here with a couple of his men and disposed of the coins. He wrote the location down in a set of cryptic clues that would lead him back at a later date but would be meaningless to anyone else. Then, before he could come back, he and many of his men were killed in the Battle of Québec. Since that time, no one has been able to decipher the clues and recover the stash."

"Until you came along," Addie said, unconvinced.

"Right." Cam had unpacked the tent and was busy putting it up in the glow of his flashlight. He looked up at Addie. "Any more questions?"

"No." Addie figured that once they poked around the woods for a couple of days and found nothing, Cam would come to his senses, and they could hike back down to the trailhead. In the meantime, she would get to enjoy some alone time with him free of cell phones, the internet, and all the other distractions that vied for his attention back on campus. Not to mention the professor, who took up more than his fair share of Cam's time with his boring and pointless history project chasing Captain McAllister all over Maine. "Is there anything I can do to help?"

"Yes." Cam nodded. "Gather some wood to build a fire."

Addie looked around, nervous. "On my own?"

"One of us has to put the tent up." There was a note of exasperation in Cam's voice. "Don't tell me those guys down the trail got you spooked with their talk of monsters."

"No." Addie shook her head. "Don't be silly."

"Good." Cam was banging tent pegs into the ground with a small rubber mallet. "Then what are you waiting for? It's freezing out here. Go find some wood and let's build a fire!"

TWENTY-FIVE

AN HOUR after their encounter with the hikers, Decker found Strand standing at the edge of the clearing, gazing along the trail with his hands pushed into his pockets and a thoughtful look on his face.

"You look troubled," Decker said as he drew close.

Strand never took his eyes off the trail. "Just wondering about our two friends."

"You sensed it too, huh?"

"They were acting shifty. Even after we told them it wasn't safe, they were dead set on continuing."

"You think they're up to something?"

Strand shrugged. "I don't know. It's just a feeling."

"Maybe they just wanted privacy. A couple of kids that age, out on their own with no one around for miles . . .?" Decker followed Strand's gaze. The trail curved a few hundred feet from their vantage point, then switched back on itself. Even though the hikers had said their camp was not far away, there was no sign of them.

"Except us." Strand turned back toward the camp. "You're probably right. I just hope they don't get into trouble up there."

"Me too." Decker walked with Strand back toward the fire where the others were gathered. They were about to spend their second night in the wilderness, and he hoped it would be less eventful than the first. Earlier that day, they had repositioned the trail cameras, placing one near the stream where they had found the footprint and moving the others deeper into the surrounding Woodland. With any luck, one of the units would capture an image to prove one way or the other what was roaming around. Then again, maybe they wouldn't record anything out of the ordinary. Because Decker had been thinking about how the creature had gotten so close the previous night and tripped none of the trail cameras placed around the camp at intervals, specifically for that purpose. Now, he was beginning to form a theory based on an idea that had flitted tantalizingly out of reach at the back of his mind since the day before. A theory that could explain the strange events. Except he wasn't sure how to prove his fledgling hunch. He sat down and stared across the fire at Norwood, who had his nose in a tattered old paperback book.

Norwood sensed he was being studied and looked up. "What?"

"Nothing." Decker pulled his gaze away.

"You alright, there?" Strand asked, taking a seat next to Decker.

"Yes. Why?"

"Because I can see the cogs moving in that brain of yours. Want to share?"

Decker shook his head. "Not yet."

"Well, don't leave it too long. I don't like being kept in the dark, especially when my ass is on the line."

"Understood." Decker's gaze shifted back toward Norwood, who was reading his book again, and wondered if his hunch was correct.

TWENTY-SIX

ADDIE WELLS LAY with the sleeping bag pulled up to her chin and waited for Cam to finish playing with his phone. It was gone one in the morning, and she had been hoping he would pay attention to her instead of staring at that stupid screen for an hour. It was made worse because there wasn't even any service, which meant no internet.

"What are you doing?" She asked for the fifth time, not bothering to hide the annoyance in her voice now.

"You know what I'm doing." Cam glanced sideways toward her, making eye contact for a moment before his gaze returned to the phone and the photos he had taken when they broke into Professor Calloway's office. Photos of documents that Calloway guarded with a zeal that would have seemed odd had it not been for the secret hidden within the dusty old paperwork. "I want to start searching for McAllister's ill-gotten loot first thing in the morning and I don't want to waste my time searching in the wrong place."

"We came here to this spot because you claimed it was the

right place," Addie said, reaching out from her sleeping bag and touching his arm. "Were you wrong?"

"No. I'm not wrong." Cam was sitting up with his own sleeping bag bunched around his waist. He barely seemed to notice the nippy air inside the tent, despite wearing only a thin cotton top. "But it's still a large search area."

"Speaking of which, what exactly are we searching for? I mean, did McAllister bury a chest like some kind of pirate?"

Cam laughed. "Not so much." He glanced toward a folding metal detector that he'd brought up to the camping site inside his backpack. "It would have been a wooden box for sure, but nothing like a pirate's chest. Much smaller. Probably about the size of a shoebox. Of course, by now the box has probably rotted away, leaving just the coins and maybe a few old nails and pieces of hardware."

"And you're going to find it with that thing?" Addie glanced toward the metal detector.

"It's about the only way we can find those coins. They should be the only metal things up here."

"Right. Except for a couple hundred years of littering by explorers, fur trappers, and hikers. I can't wait to find all those soda cans tomorrow."

"Soda cans are aluminum. We'll be looking for silver, copper, and bronze. We can discriminate against aluminum since it wasn't even around back then."

"Wow. You're really leaning into this." Addie raised an eyebrow. "Where did you even get a metal detector?"

"Where do you think? I bought it online."

"Great. That puts us a couple hundred bucks in the hole right from the start."

"And if we find the loot McAllister stole from the Continental Army, we'll be hundreds of thousands in the green."

"For some copper and bronze?" Addie snorted. "Silver isn't even worth that much. Maybe if it was gold coins."

"Gold coins were super rare in the colonies. And you're right, the copper and bronze coins probably aren't worth a bundle. But if McAllister's papers are correct, there were some silver coins mixed in. According to McAllister, at least a few of them were 'pine tree shillings' minted decades earlier for the Massachusetts Bay Colony by a merchant named John Hull. Super rare. Just one of those shillings could fetch a quarter million at auction."

"And we're just going to steal them out from under the professor?"

"We're not stealing anything. The coins have been out here for hundreds of years, just waiting to be found. I'm the one who cracked McAllister's code and figured out where he buried them. Besides, if Calloway gets his hands on the coins, he'll just donate them to the university, or maybe the state. That money could set us up for life. Pay off our student loans. Buy us a house."

"I suppose." Addie wasn't sure she agreed with what they were doing. She had assumed that the buried coins might be worth several thousand dollars. Maybe enough to pay for college. Now she found out that just two of the coins might be worth a combined half a million or more. It crossed the line from an adventure to what felt like looting. But it was too late now. Then another thought occurred to her. "Is this even legal? We're on public land."

"All above board." Cam finally put the phone down. "When we find those coins--"

"If we find them . . ."

"We will! And when we do, we'll report our discovery as treasure trove, and it will belong to us. Easy. The professor and university won't have a claim, nor will the state."

"I don't know." Addie didn't think that sounded right, but she also wasn't a lawyer.

"So worried. This time next week, we might be rolling in dough." Cam climbed out of his sleeping bag and scooted over toward her, then unzipped her sleeping bag. "In the meantime, we can keep each other warm."

"That sounds nice." Addie let him climb in with her and waited for him to zip the sleeping bag back up. There was barely any room and his body pressed against hers. She felt his hand run down her back, toward her waist, and slip inside the stretch cotton shorts she had worn to bed. He started sliding them down. "Hey. I thought you just wanted to keep warm."

"I never said how I want to keep warm." Cam grinned.

"Cut it out." Addie wormed an arm into the sleeping bag and made a token effort to stop him even as his other hand tugged at her top. She was about to admonish him again, more halfheartedly this time, when the sharp crack of a twig snapping somewhere outside made them both stop in their tracks.

TWENTY-SEVEN

"WHAT WAS THAT?" Addie sat up quickly, dragging Cam along with her as she pulled her top back down. "It sounded close."

"Probably just an animal wandering close to the camp." Cam rubbed her back. "Don't worry about it."

"You think?"

"I'm sure."

Addie relaxed. The group camping further down the trail had her all jumpy with their talk of a Sasquatch running around, which was, of course, ridiculous. If it was that easy to see a Bigfoot, they would have been discovered long before now, right? She was about to recline and scoot back inside the sleeping bag when it came again.

A sharp snap, closer to the tent this time.

Addie couldn't help a small whimper. "Whatever it is, it doesn't sound like it's going away."

Cam rolled his eyes. "We're in the woods. What do you expect?"

"I don't know. What do you think it is?"

"Could be a moose or a bear. Maybe even a deer." Cam thought for a moment. "It could even be those guys down the trail trying to scare us."

"You think so?"

"Wouldn't put it past them. After all, they did try to convince us that a Bigfoot was roaming around the woods." Cam let out a laugh that sounded more like a snort. "Idiots. I bet they're up here looking for McAllister's loot, too. That would explain the ridiculous story. Probably figure they can chase us away. Just a couple of dumb kids. Well, the joke's on them. I'm not going anywhere, not until we've--"

Another sound from outside drifted into the tent, interrupting Cam's indignant tirade. This time, it wasn't a twig. It was a shuffling, rustling noise, like . . .

"Something is sniffing around the camp." Addie stared at the tent flap with wide-eyed fear. "You remembered to put the supplies away after dinner, right?"

"Of course I did." Cam turned and patted his backpack. "Everything is safe and sound in here."

The rustling came again.

Addie shrank back. "I'm scared. What if it tries to get in here?"

"It won't."

"You don't know that. We have a fire going. That should keep the animals away but obviously whatever is out there doesn't care."

"Oh, for heaven's sake." Cam pushed himself out of the sleeping bag and half stood, grabbing his pants. He put them on and buckled them, then found a sweater and pulled it over his head. "Stay here. I'll go take a look. Will that make you happy?"

"Don't go out there," Addie hissed under her breath. "It might not be safe."

"You'd rather sit here and see if our nocturnal visitor tries to get in the tent?"

"I didn't say that. I just don't want you to--"

"I'll be fine." Cam reached into his backpack and pulled out a flashlight. Then he unzipped the tent and crawled out into the night before zipping it up again. His voice drifted back through the thin tent fabric. "I don't see anything in the camp. I'm sure it was just a deer or something. I'll take a quick look around and I'll be back."

"No." The last thing Addie wanted was to be left alone. But it was too late. Cam didn't reply. Instead, she heard his footsteps padding away across the campsite, and then she was left in silence.

TWENTY-EIGHT

BARRY NORWOOD LAY in his tent and stared into the darkness. It was one in the morning, and he couldn't sleep. It seemed like whenever he came to this spot in the Maine woods, he relived the same waking nightmare.

Bigfoot was out there.

He knew it as surely as he knew his own name. He'd seen it when he was a kid. The creature had scared the living daylights out of him. Then he let his friends talk him into coming back to this spot and it had ended with them having to carry one of their own out on a makeshift stretcher. Now these strangers had convinced him to come back here once more, and it was starting all over again. The night before, something had thrown stones at the tents. When they went into the woods to investigate, it was out there waiting for them. A man named Decker and his scary sidekick with the special forces vibes, Strand, had come face to face with the beast. They had almost died. Coming here was a bad idea. In the morning, he would insist that they leave. Hike back down to their SUV and get far away from this dreadful place. And if Decker and his pals protested, refused to go, then that was their choice. Either way, Norwood was done. Now all he had to do was get through the rest of the night and try to stop obsessing about that horrid creature.

TWENTY-NINE

A QUARTER OF AN HOUR PASSED, and Cam was not back. Addie sat in the tent with the sleeping bag pulled up to her chin and tried not to think about what might be out there. Was it a wild animal, or was it those guys down the trail trying to scare them off? Either way, her boyfriend should be back by now.

Addie could stand it no longer. The silence was deafening. Where was Cam? She leaned forward, close to the tent flap where he had vanished, and called out in a half whisper.

"Cam, are you still out there?"

No answer.

Addie swallowed the lump that had formed in her throat, took a deep breath to steady her nerves. She called out again and received nothing in response. Her stomach clenched. She pushed the sleeping bag off her legs and unzipped the flap. Then she paused, afraid to see what might be out there. Then another thought entered her head and spurred her to action. Was Cam somewhere outside, lying injured, the victim of whatever had invaded their campsite?

Maybe he hadn't answered because he couldn't.

Pushing her fear down deep, Addie pulled the tent flaps back and slowly, almost unwillingly, poked her head outside.

Nothing.

The camp was still. Empty. The fire had burned down, the flames a mere shadow of what they had been hours before. Soon, if more wood was not added, it would go out.

Addie climbed from the tent and stood up. She looked around, hoping to see Cam somewhere close by, maybe standing between the trees, or out by the trail, yet still didn't see him.

This was bad.

Scratch that. It was beyond bad. How far could he have gone? And why would he leave her vulnerable and alone?

"Cam?" She called louder this time. "I don't like this. Where are you?"

This time, instead of silence, she got a response. Somewhere behind her, in the darkness behind the tent, someone was moving, coming closer.

Addie's heart leaped. It must be Cam coming back to the campsite. Any moment now, he would appear from between the trees and tell her that it was nothing to worry about. Just a deer, or maybe a porcupine out for a late-night stroll. She took a step toward the sound, ready to greet him, and then she froze. Because the figure that emerged from the woods was not Cam. In fact, it was unlike anything Addie had ever seen. And the smell . . . Foul. Putrescent. It made her eyes water, even as she stared in disbelief. For a moment, Addie was paralyzed, unable to move, as the creature stepped from between the trees and shambled closer, fixing her with luminous yellow eyes that burned with malevolence. Then, with a terrified screech, she found the will to run.

THIRTY

DECKER SAT CLOSE to the fire with the rifle across his lap. It was two in the morning, and so far all was quiet. They had heard nothing from either the two hikers further up the trail, or their unfriendly visitor from the night before. The evening had passed without incident, and when it came time to retire a little before midnight, Decker suggested that he and Strand take turns keeping watch again. If anything happened, he wanted to be ready this time. Which was why he volunteered to take the first shift, from midnight until four A.M.

Now, with nothing to do but stare off into the darkness and wait, he felt his eyelids drooping. Which was why he stoked the fire and made a pot of what Strand referred to as cowboy coffee, which was really just brewed in the camping coffee percolator rather than the true definition that required boiling grounds in a heavy pot.

After two steaming mugs, his mojo returned. He felt alert and ready for whatever might come his way. And for the first couple of hours, nothing did. But then, just as he was falling

ANTHONY M. STRONG

into a false sense of security, wondering if the creature they had encountered the previous night wasn't going to make an encore, a small stone came sailing out of the woods and landed on the soft earth a few feet away from him.

Decker sprang to his feet.

He brought the rifle up and scanned the gloom between the trees.

The hairs on the back of his neck prickled. He could sense the creature watching him, even if he couldn't see it.

A rustle of leaves.

Decker tensed, his index finger hovering above the rifle's trigger. He considered alerting Strand, who currently had the Glock pistol, but he didn't know how to do so without spooking whatever was there.

A second stone sailed through the air, coming closer to the tents this time but still falling short. Decker calculated the trajectory. It originated more to the left. The creature was circling, possibly summing up the situation.

Decker kept the rifle leveled and took a few steps toward the forest.

More rustling.

A twig snapped, the sound sharp and quick.

"You see anything?"

The hushed voice from behind Decker sent his heart crashing against his ribs. He took a deep breath to steady his nerves. The unexpected voice belonged to Strand, who must have been roused by the beast's arrival, anyway.

Decker shook his head. "Too dark. But it's out there."

"Didn't mean to scare you," Strand whispered, taking a position at Decker's left shoulder. The Glock was in his hand.

"I wasn't expecting anyone to sneak up behind me, that's all," Decker replied. His racing heart had calmed now. "Why are you awake, anyway?"

112

"Never went to sleep. Figured we might get a return visit."

"So you just sat in your tent and waited?"

"Something like that." Strand's gaze swept the boundary where the trees met the clearing.

"You could've come out and kept me company."

"Nah. Figured that might keep our nocturnal visitor away. Too much activity. You were better as bait."

"Thanks."

"Don't mention it." Strand turned to check their rear. "It's all quiet now. You think it left?"

"Beats me," Decker replied. "Only one way to find out."

"Go take a look?"

"Precisely." Decker started toward the trees.

"Want to swap weapons?" Strand asked as they went. He looked down at the Glock. "I like the rifle better."

Decker fixed him with a sideways stare but said nothing.

"Hey. Just a suggestion. It is my gun, after all."

"Not right now, it's not." They stepped out of the clearing and into the woods. The trees pressed around them on all sides.

"Figured as much." Strand took a pair of compact LED flashlights from his pocket. He handed one to Decker and kept the other for himself.

"Thanks." Decker took the flashlight and clicked it on. He pushed through a tangle of underbrush, looking left and right. "The last stone came from somewhere around here."

"There's nothing here now," said Strand, sweeping their surroundings with his own flashlight.

"I see that."

"Maybe we scared it away." Strand scratched his head. "Let's do a turn around the perimeter and make sure it isn't circling back on us."

"Good idea."

They started off, pushing through the understory and following parallel to the edge of the clearing. They heard nothing larger than a raccoon scrabbling out of the way as they went. If the creature was still lurking in the undergrowth, it didn't want to be found.

After a while, they came upon the trail leading further into the woods.

Decker stepped out from under the cover of trees and was about to cross over when he sensed movement from the corner of his eye. He swiveled, bringing the rifle around. The blood rushed in his ears. An explosion of adrenaline coursed through him. His finger curled around the trigger.

To his right, he sensed Strand turn in surprise. He lifted the Glock and dropped into a two-handed firing stance.

"Wait." Decker lowered the rifle.

It wasn't a wild animal coming down the trail toward them, no lumbering beast with malice in its eyes.

It was the woman they had encountered earlier in the evening, hiking up the trail with her boyfriend. Except now she was alone . . . and running for her life.

THIRTY-ONE

THE WOMAN STUMBLED down the path toward them, eyes wild, an expression of horror on her face. She was wearing a tank top and stretch cotton shorts, a pajama outfit she had clearly been sleeping in. Her hair billowed out behind her in blonde waves.

Decker sprinted to meet the distressed woman. He recalled that her name was Addie but couldn't remember her boyfriend's name.

"Help me, please," she said, her voice full of panic.

"What happened?" Decker asked as she drew close.

Strand had another question. "Where's your companion? The man you came out here with."

"I don't know." Addie was close to tears. "We were in the tent, and something came into our camp. He went to see what it was and never came back . . ."

"Take it easy," Decker said, as the young woman practically fell into his arms. "You're safe now."

"None of us are safe." Addie was sucking in mouthfuls of

the frosty night air. Goosebumps rose all along her bare arms. "I saw it."

"Saw what?" Strand asked.

"The Bigfoot. It's real, just like you said. I went to find Cam when he didn't return, and there it was. Standing at the edge of the campsite. It was looking right at me." She gave a choking sob. "Oh God, I think it killed Cam."

"All right. Let's get you back to our camp," Decker said, putting a guiding hand around her shoulder. He could feel her shivering under his touch. She was not dressed for a chilly winter night in Maine. "We'll get you warmed up."

"No. We have to look for Cam." She pulled back against Decker's arm.

"Not until we take care of you." Decker steered her back down the trail toward the clearing. "You can tell us everything that happened, and then we'll look for him. I promise."

"Okay." Addie nodded, but she sounded unsure. Even so, she let Decker lead her back to their camp and toward the fire.

Decker threw another couple of logs on, along with some smaller branches. As the flames leaped higher, she warmed herself and the shivering slowly abated. He went to his tent and ducked inside, coming out with a pair of clean jeans and a heavy coat, which he offered to her.

"Here. Put these on. They might be a little big on you, but they're better than nothing."

"Thank you." Addie grabbed the clothing and quickly donned it. She flicked her hair back over the coat collar and wiped her eyes.

"What's going on?" Norwood appeared from his tent, closely followed by Levesque.

"We found her on the trail." Strand was keeping a wary eye on the dark woods.

Decker could tell he was antsy to go look for Cam. But first, they needed Addie to tell them everything. Decker looked at her. "Now, start from the beginning."

Addie nodded. "Okay. I'll do my best." She paused and took a deep breath. "We were in the tent and Cam was wanting to . . ." She stopped again, a blush touching her cheeks. "Anyway, that doesn't matter. We were just settling down when there was a noise outside. It sounded like an animal foraging through our camp. Cam told me to stay where I was, then he got dressed and went to see what it was. At first, I could hear him outside, walking around, but then it went quiet. I sat there waiting for him to come back and he didn't. I unzipped the tent flap and called his name, but he didn't answer . . ."

"It's okay, take your time."

Addie bit her lip. She made a visible effort to compose herself. "I climbed out of the tent to look for him, but the campsite was empty, and it was so dark. Then there was this horrible smell, and the weirdest feeling came over me like I was being watched."

Decker and Strand exchanged a glance.

Norwood and Levesque were watching the woman intently.

"Go on," said Decker.

Addie wiped a tear from her cheek. "At first I couldn't see anything out of place, but then I saw it at the edge of the camp. This huge hairy creature. It was standing upright on two legs, and it was so tall. Like seven feet or more."

"What happened next?" Levesque asked. He licked his lips and gulped.

"It was just watching me and there was no sign of Cam."

Addie squeezed her eyes closed, then opened them again. "It made this horrible grunting sound and started walking toward me. I panicked. I just turned and ran down the trail. That's when I found you guys." Her voice cracked. "Oh my God. I abandoned Cam. I left him up there all alone to die."

"To be clear, you didn't actually see his body?" Strand asked.

Decker shot him a disapproving glance, but Addie didn't appear to notice. She shook her head. "I didn't see him at all. I don't know where he was. But if he's up there with that monster, he must be dead."

"We have to find this woman's boyfriend and take care of this once and for all," Decker said, looking around the group. "Are we all agreed?"

One by one, everyone nodded.

"Good." Decker steered Addie to a chair and told her to sit down. Then he turned to Levesque. "How are you with a gun?"

"Good enough."

"Wonderful." Decker took the Glock from Strand and handed it to Levesque. "You're going to stay here with Addie and make sure nothing happens to her."

"Don't you think I should come with you?" Levesque asked, although with little enthusiasm. "I am the zoologist here. If there's an unknown animal running around, you might need my expertise."

"Right now, all we need is your tranquilizer gun," said Decker, giving the rifle to Strand, who was probably the better shot. "I'd rather not go out there completely unarmed."

"I can stay here if you want," said Norwood. "Wouldn't that make more sense?"

Decker shook his head. "I want you with us."

"Why?"

"Not now. We don't have the time." He turned to Levesque. "Get me the tranquilizer gun and darts. Hurry."

Levesque disappeared toward his tent. He returned a few moments later carrying the air rifle and a small plastic pouch containing four slim tranquilizer darts with orange tassels on one end. He handed it to Decker. "I loaded a dart in the gun already. If you need to reload, just pull the bolt back and drop another dart in, then close and lock it again. It's a little finicky but you'll get the hang of it. I set the gun at the highest velocity already. Figured you'll want that if you come face to face with whatever is out there."

"Good job," Decker said, taking the gun and darts. He took Levesque to one side, far enough away that the others wouldn't hear their conversation. A minute later, satisfied with what he'd learned, Decker returned to the group. He kneeled next to Addie. "We'll find him."

Addie sniffed and nodded but said nothing.

Decker straightened and set his sights on the trail leading further into the woods. He hitched the air rifle over his shoulder, pushed the darts into his pocket, and started off into the night. "Let's go find ourselves a Sasquatch."

THIRTY-TWO

THEY TRUDGED up the path toward the higher camp where Addie and Cam had settled earlier that evening. It was a moonless night with a thick layer of cloud cover that drenched the landscape in inky blackness.

Strand went first, carrying the rifle, with Norwood in the middle and Decker bringing up the rear with the tranquilizer gun.

The beams from their flashlights illuminated little more than a small patch of ground a few feet ahead. Enough to navigate, but not to see any dangers that lurked within the woods on either side. Like a seven-foot-tall allegedly mythical ape with a bad attitude.

"Keep sharp, men," said Strand, sweeping his flashlight from side to side and observing their surroundings with a wary eye.

"Do either of you actually have a plan if we meet the Bigfoot?" Norwood asked. "Because I can tell you, that creature is not friendly. Look what it did to Big Willie."

"Seriously. You really call him that?" Strand looked at Norwood. "A grown man?"

"Started when he was in high school and kind of stuck. Not that you'd dare say it if you aren't his bud."

"Ridiculous." Strand snorted and turned his attention back to the trail.

"Woods are thinning out ahead," said Decker, noticing how the trail was opening up into another clearing of sorts smaller than their own camp.

"This must be the place." Strand pointed to a green two-person tent and a smoldering fire dug into a pit. A backpack sat by the fire, next to a pair of camping chairs, one of which was toppled on its side. The side of the tent was slashed open. One pole was bent. The center sagged inward. "Guess that whatever came for a visit wasn't in a good mood."

"Our missing hiker could be anywhere," Decker said, studying their surroundings. "Quicker we start looking, the faster we can get back to our own camp."

"Agreed." Strand took a step toward the tent.

A low animalistic growl drifted from the woods.

All three turned toward the noise.

"You think that was a racoon?" Decker asked.

"Nope." Strand lifted the rifle.

"Me either." Decker motioned for Norwood to move behind them and dropped the air rifle from his shoulder. There was one dart loaded already, but once he fired, it would take precious seconds to reload. He hoped he wouldn't need to.

A rock sailed out of the understory and whizzed past Decker's ear, falling to the ground near the destroyed tent.

"Our visitor from last night is definitely back," Strand said.

"Kind of a unique calling card." Decker felt his gut

tighten. The last time they encountered this creature up close it had not gone well. He didn't hold out much hope it would go any better this time.

He was right.

Before anyone had time to react, the brush parted, and the Sasquatch raced toward them with an angry howl. It was just as big as Decker remembered from the night before, with coarse black hair and an impossibly large head sitting on a thick neck.

"Holy hell." Strand raised the rifle and fired without taking time to aim.

The creature flinched but kept coming.

Strand fired again at point-blank range.

There was no way he could have missed at such a distance, but he might as well have been swatting at it with a rolled-up newspaper.

Decker lifted the air rifle and squeezed the trigger. A dart sailed toward the beast. The projectile lodged in the creature's chest.

The beast brought a hand up and swatted it loose with a bellow.

"This isn't working." Strand backed up, almost bowling over Norwood, who appeared rooted to the spot, eyes fixed on the fast-approaching beast.

The bump galvanized him, and he did the same.

Decker didn't have the time to reload and wasn't sure it would do any good, even if he did. He retreated back toward the torn tent and weighed their options at the same time, which weren't good.

Even if they turned and fled, the creature was clearly fast. Too quick to outrun. It would be mere seconds before one or more of them ended up like Big Willie . . . or worse. Standing their ground was obviously out, too. They were stuck in an impossible situation.

"How did my rifle not bring that thing down?" Strand hollered as they reached the edge of the camp.

"I think I know why," Decker answered, "but I'm not sure what to do about it."

"Mind sharing?"

"I think we have bigger problems right now." Decker raised the useless gun as the creature closed the gap, intending to use it as a club. He tensed, waiting for the inevitable collision as the Bigfoot caught them.

But then, from across the clearing, he heard a new voice.

"Hey, ugly. Over here." It was Cam. He appeared from the woods, wearing a torn and filthy pair of jeans and tee. He waved to attract the creature's attention. For a moment Decker didn't understand what he was doing, but then realization dawned. He was trying to buy them time to escape.

The creature stopped, gave a frustrated shriek, and changed direction.

"No. Don't do that," Decker shouted, waving at Cam. "You can't outrun it."

"Already have once today." Cam darted around the side of the clearing, keeping close to the trees.

"You don't understand." Decker felt a stab of fear. He knew why Cam had escaped the beast, and it wouldn't happen this time.

"It will rip him to shreds," Strand said, raising his rifle. "We have to draw that creature's attention back to us."

"Do it. I have a plan." Decker was fumbling to reload the air rifle with a new dart and making a hash of it. He had never used a modified weapon such as this before.

"Like to share?"

"No time. Just keep the damned thing occupied."

"You'd better know what you're doing." Strand rushed forward and fired off another shot as he went. His aim was wide, but it had the desired effect.

The creature changed direction a second time, barreling back toward the trio.

"Oh, hell." Strand turned and ran back toward the trail, leading the beast away from Decker and Norwood. But he was outmatched. The Sasquatch was gaining on him. Fast.

Another moment and he would be done for.

Decker pushed the thought from his mind and concentrated on the job at hand. Finally, and much to his relief, he got the dart loaded.

Now he took aim. But not at the creature.

Decker adjusted the rifle's power to its lowest setting, backed up several steps to put some distance between them, and fired point-blank at Norwood.

THIRTY-THREE

A FLASH of surprise registered on Norwood's face as Decker turned and fired.

He raised his arms in defense. "What are you—"

The dart smacked home, hitting Norwood in the upper left thigh. Decker had chosen the spot because he felt it was the safest location to shoot him.

"Ow." Norwood staggered backward and tugged at the dart, pulling it free, but it was already too late. The projectile's contents, a sedative intended to subdue large animals, were already working their way through his bloodstream.

"Whatever you're doing, better make it quick." Strand was at the edge of the clearing and barely ahead of the creature now.

Decker had done all he could. He only hoped his hunch was correct, and that he'd done everything right.

Norwood was staggering now, his eyes taking on a glazed sheen. He took a faltering step, then another. His eyelids fluttered. Then he crumpled to the ground.

ANTHONY M. STRONG

Across the clearing, Strand was in trouble. The creature reached out with a long muscular arm and swatted at him, sending the Ghost Team operative tumbling sideways.

He lost his footing and fell, scrambling backward as the Sasquatch turned to finish the job with a triumphant roar.

But instead of attacking, the creature paused, shaking its head from side to side as if confused. Then, as Decker watched, it started to pull apart as if made of nothing more than smoke. Long coils of wispy matter spiraled up from the beast, twisting into the air and dissipating in the wind. Soon it was nothing more than a faint outline against the darker backdrop of the forest, and then it was gone, as if it had never existed at all.

THIRTY-FOUR

DECKER RUSHED OVER to Norwood and kneeled beside him, checking his vitals. He was relieved to find a strong pulse.

Strand climbed to his feet and brushed himself off. He rubbed his shoulder with a grimace and made his way toward Decker. "Landed on this funny. I'm going to have a bruise or two tomorrow."

"Better than the alternative," Decker said, glancing up as the Ghost Team operative reached him.

"Right." Strand looked down at the sedated Norwood. "Is he going to be all right?"

"Hope so." Decker had taken Levesque aside before they went looking for Cam and quizzed him about the sedative in the darts. According to the zoologist, there were several types of animal tranquilizers, most of which were extremely dangerous to humans, and could even cause death. But at least one had been used on people as an anesthetic in the past. Decker was pleased to learn that this was what the dart contained. Still, the dosage had to be correct. Too much could still have fatal consequences, while too little would do nothing but give Norwood a bad trip.

If his hunch about the Sasquatch was correct, Decker needed Norwood out cold. To this end he had drained as much sedative from the dart as he dared before using it, erring on the side of giving a lower dose than needed. Luckily, he made the right decision.

"You made a hell of a judgment call shooting him with that dart," Strand said. "Even at that air rifle's lowest setting, you ran the risk of causing severe injury."

"That's why I shot him in the thigh from as far away as I dared," Decker said. "I would've preferred putting the dart in his butt, but there wasn't time to explain the situation and ask him to turn around."

Cam was approaching the group with a worried look on his face. "We have to find my girlfriend."

"She's safe," Strand told him. "Addie's at our campsite."

"Oh, thank God. I was so worried." Cam slumped visibly. "What the hell just happened here?"

Strand folded his arms and looked at Decker. "I'd like to know that, too. Whatever possessed you to shoot this man with a tranquilizer dart, and how could it make the Sasquatch disappear?"

"Because it wasn't really a Sasquatch," Decker said.

"Right." Cam didn't look convinced. "Looked like a real Sasquatch when it was trying to kill me."

"Nevertheless, it was no such thing." Decker stood.

"Then what was it?"

"A Tulpa."

"A what, now?" Cam shook his head. "Never heard of it."

"I have," said Strand. "A thought-form made real by the belief of its creator."

"Exactly." Decker looked down at Norwood, who was

still out for the count, but looked fine otherwise. "Barry Norwood's father brought him out here to camp when he was a young boy. The old man reveled in scaring his son with campfire tales. All manner of ghouls and creepy things. But one story in particular stuck with the kid. A tale his father swore was true about seeing the Bigfoot when he himself was a boy camping with Barry's grandfather. It terrified him to the point of obsession. Whenever he would come up here with his dad, Barry would lay awake for hours in the darkness wondering if the Sasquatch was coming for him."

"And eventually it did," Strand interjected.

"Right. He heard a noise one night and peeked out of his tent to see the Bigfoot standing in their campsite, just like his father claimed to have seen before him. It wasn't real, of course. At least, not in the true sense of the word. It was a projection of his mind."

Strand looked between the two men. "His fear externally manifested right in front of him."

"Fine." Cam still didn't look convinced. "He scared himself to death as a kid and created an imaginary creature. How does that explain what's happening here and now?"

"It wasn't imaginary. It might have started out that way, but it took on a corporeal presence. Belief can be a powerful thing."

"You think that coming up here as an adult with his friends reignited that fear," Strand said.

"That's exactly what I think happened. They made him recount the tale of his Bigfoot encounter and those old fears resurfaced. He projected it into life once again to terrorize them."

Strand nodded in agreement. "Likewise, when we brought him up here to investigate the encounter, the

Sasquatch returned because he expected it to. This was the place of his greatest fears."

"Which is why it faded away when you shot him with that dart," Cam said.

Now Decker nodded. "Without Barry Norwood's active mind to create the Tulpa, it could no longer hold a physical presence."

"Which means that . . ." Cam's gaze fell to the snoozing Norwood.

"If he wakes up, the creature will return." Decker completed the half-formed sentence.

"In that case, we'd better get him back to our campsite quick as we can, and out of these woods at first light," Strand said. "I'm not sure we'll survive another encounter with that beast."

"Agreed," Decker said. He turned to Cam. "Not to mention that there's a young woman who will be overjoyed to see you alive and well."

"I'm looking forward to seeing her, too," Cam replied. "When that creature chased me out of the camp I tried to get back to her, did everything I could to keep her safe."

"We believe you," said Decker.

Cam nodded. He glanced down at Norwood. "Umm . . . How are we going to get this man out of here? Doesn't look like he's in any condition to walk out under his own steam."

"Which is why we'll need a volunteer to carry him," Decker said, "and failing that, I guess we'll have to draw straws."

THIRTY-FIVE

THREE DAYS LATER-BELFAST, MAINE

"SASQUATCHES AREN'T REAL," Norwood said, with an almost palpable disappointment in his tone.

"I don't know if they're real or not," Decker replied. "But the one that plagued you was nothing more than a creation of your own mind."

They were sitting in the living room of Norwood's apartment. Decker was conducting what his boss at Classified Universal Special Projects, Adam Hunt, called an informal debrief. "I don't understand how you knew," Norwood said. "I mean, not even I was aware of what was really going on."

"It's my job to know. But more to the point, I simply applied logical deduction."

"Meaning?"

"The reports of a Bigfoot showing up in that area whenever you were there were too predictable, given the elusive nature of the beast in question. You had an encounter at that campsite when you were a boy after your father told you stories of the Bigfoot. When you returned as an adult, convinced to return by your friends, the creature also made a comeback with results that could have proved fatal. Likewise, when you accompanied us to the same spot, the Sasquatch showed up yet again each night we were there."

"You're saying it was too much of a coincidence?"

"Yes. A little research told me that there have been no other reliable Sasquatch sightings in that area except yours. The common denominator in every incident was your presence."

Norwood looked unsure. "But it went away when you sedated me."

"Exactly. Because your active mind was disengaged," Decker said.

"So how come it appeared in the middle of the night when everyone was sleeping?"

"Ah, but it didn't appear when *everyone* was sleeping. I'll wager that you were awake on each occasion, or at least not fully asleep."

"I did find it hard to sleep up there in the woods for sure. I would lay awake in my tent for hours. All I could think about was the Bigfoot."

"And there you have it," said Decker. He stood up, feeling that this brought the conversation to a neat close.

But Norwood still had questions. "What if you were wrong, and I wasn't creating the beast? What if it wasn't a Tulpa, but something else entirely?"

"Then we would have been in a heap of trouble," Decker admitted. "For a while there, the answer was nagging at the back of my mind, but I couldn't reel it in. After I took a step back and assessed the evidence, it came to me. There was only one logical explanation."

"The Sasquatch was a creation of my own fears."

Decker nodded.

"You took a colossal risk."

"I made a judgment call. It turned out to be the correct one."

"Thank goodness."

"Thank goodness, indeed," Decker repeated. He turned toward the door. "If we have any more questions, we'll be in touch. I'll see myself out."

"Wait." Norwood jumped to his feet.

Decker turned back to face him. "Is there something else?"

"The Sasquatch. It's still there, hiding inside my subconscious. How can I make sure it never returns?"

"Easy," Decker replied with a smile. "Don't go camping."

EPILOGUE

SIX MONTHS LATER

ADDIE WELLS STOOD at the edge of the clearing and watched as the top layer of dirt was excavated in a taped off area deep in the Maine wilderness by a contingent of Central Maine University students wielding small trowels and brushes. They were at the site where she and Cam had set up camp months before. It was also the spot where her boyfriend had almost died at the hands of an unknown creature that everyone later claimed was a bear foraging for food prior to hibernation. That wasn't the truth, of course. But the man named John Decker and his scary companion, Philip Strand, had made it clear that they were not to reveal what really occurred on that frosty November night. What would happen if they did talk was anyone's guess, but she didn't want to find out. Besides, there was no point. No one would believe them.

"Isn't this great?" Cam appeared from between the trees and came bounding toward her, a wide grin on his face.

"If you say so." Addie glanced toward the row of tents set up in what was now a much larger clearing. One of them belonged to her and Cam. She still didn't enjoy camping much, even though it was now May, which meant there was no snow on the ground and the temperature had risen to a more bearable fifty degrees.

"Come on, don't be such a stick in the mud." Cam put his arm around her waist. "Everything worked out in the end. Although I'm still not sure why I let you convince me to tell Professor Calloway about my discovery instead of coming back up here on our own for McAllister's loot."

"Because deep down you're a nice guy," Addie said, returning the hug. "Once you took a step back and looked at it rationally, you realized it was the right thing to do."

"Yeah. Whatever. I'm never admitting that we broke into his office, though."

"That goes without saying." Addie glanced back toward the dig site as a chorus of excited chatter erupted from inside the taped off area. The students were huddled over a recently dug trench and at first she couldn't see what all the fuss was about. But then, Professor Calloway emerged from the group and started toward them with a grin on his face.

"You have to see this," he said, drawing close. His left hand was bunched into a fist and when he opened it, Addie saw a small round dirt encrusted object lying there.

"Is that what I think it is?" She asked, unable to contain a sudden spike of curiosity despite herself.

"Sure is. A Colonial era bronze coin."

"Wait just a minute." Cam's excitement matched that of the students moments before. "Are you telling me—"

"That we found Captain McAllister's horde?" Professor Calloway turned the coin over in his hand. The date 1756 was clearly visible. "Not necessarily. It's just one coin. But it means that someone was in this area during the correct era."

"The coins were stored in a wooden box," Addie said. "It would have rotted away. They may be scattered, so that could still be from McAllister's stolen loot."

The professor nodded. "That's what we are hoping, but the only way to know for sure is to keep excavating the site. Who knows, we may turn up the entire trove."

"Including the pine tree shillings." There was a tinge of disappointment in Cam's tone. Addie wondered if he regretted doing the right thing and telling Calloway that he had cracked the enigmatic code left behind by McAllister.

"Maybe." Calloway removed a small plastic bag from his pocket and slipped the coin inside, then sealed it. "But there's no guarantee those coins were even in the horde. It could be nothing more than fanciful details added later to spice up the story. After all, the pine tree shillings would have been minted almost a hundred years before McAllister's time. The Hull Mint stopped producing coins in 1682 when it was closed by the English government. And don't forget, silver was a rare commodity in the colonies. The likelihood that valuable and uncommon silver coins were in a horde taken from simple town folk is remote."

"But not out of the question." Addie hoped the silver coins were out there somewhere, lying just beneath the surface and waiting to be rediscovered. Regardless of whether Cam made any money off the coins, the discovery would still look good on his resume, even if he didn't appreciate it at that precise moment.

"No. It's not totally out of the question." Calloway closed his fist around the newly discovered coin, now in a protective bag, and smiled. "Stranger things have happened."

"Yes, they have." Addie stared off into the forest, and for a fleeting moment, she could have sworn she saw a pair of inhuman eyes staring back at her from between the trees. Eyes that burned a familiar yellow. She looked down quickly, overcome by a sudden sense of dread. When she looked back up, the gap between the trees was empty and she realized it had been nothing more than a trick of her overanxious imagination. The Sasquatch was gone. Banished by the man named John Decker. It hadn't even really been a Sasquatch, but rather the physical manifestation of one man's fevered nightmares brought to life by his fear. But it didn't matter. She would never forget what happened on that cold winter's night, or the creature that had lumbered out of the forest. It would haunt her forever. And here, in the place where it all happened, she had thought about barely anything else.

"Are you all right?" Cam asked, noticing the look of distress on her face.

"Yes . . . Well, no. Not really." Addie scanned the tree line one more time, then she turned away. "Can we go back to the tent? I don't like it out here right now."

"Okay." Cam exchanged a glance with the professor, then took her hand and led her toward the tent. He opened the flap and held it aside for her to enter, while behind them, at the dig site, one of the students looked up in surprise as a small stone sailed through the air from the direction of the woods and landed in the middle of the trench.

To be notified when the next book in the CUSP Files series is released, visit AnthonyMStrong.com and sign up for my mailing list.

ABOUT THE AUTHOR

Anthony M. Strong is a British-born writer living and working in the United States. He is the author of the popular John Decker series of supernatural adventure thrillers.

Anthony has worked as a graphic designer, newspaper writer, artist, and actor. When he was a young boy, he dreamed of becoming an Egyptologist and spent hours reading about pyramids and tombs. Until he discovered dinosaurs and decided to be a paleontologist instead. Neither career panned out, but he was left with a fascination for monsters and archaeology that serve him well in the John Decker books.

Anthony has traveled extensively across Europe and the United States, and weaves his love of travel into his novels, setting them both close to home and in far-off places.

Anthony currently resides most of the year on Florida's Space Coast where he can watch rockets launch from his balcony, and part of the year on an island in Maine, with his wife Sonya, and two furry bosses, Izzie and Hayden.

Connect with Anthony, find out about new releases, and get free books at **www.anthonymstrong.com**

Printed in Great Britain
by Amazon

35745460R00083